When the Man Comes Around

When the Man Comes Around

Al Lamanda

THORNDIKE PRESS
A part of Gale, a Cengage Company

GALE
A Cengage Company

GALE
A Cengage Company

Thorndike Press® Large Print Softcover Western.
This Large Print edition presents the complete and unabridged main body text of the original work as provided by the publisher and author. Supplementary sections such as illustrations, endnotes, or indexes may have been omitted to optimize the large print format.
Set in 16 pt. Plantin.

LIBRARY OF CONGRESS CIP DATA ON FILE.
CATALOGUING IN PUBLICATION FOR THIS BOOK
IS AVAILABLE FROM THE LIBRARY OF CONGRESS.

ISBN-13: 978-1-4205-3842-7 (softcover alk. paper)

Published in 2026 by arrangement with Alfred John Lamanda.

When the Man Comes Around

Chapter One

Daughtry was a small, dusty town in northern, central Texas. The railroad didn't stop there; neither did the Overland or Wells Fargo stage lines. There was no real reason to go there except to hide out from the law, which the majority of its population was.

Daughtry survived on the levy it collected from outlaws seeking a safe-haven from the law. For ten percent of whatever loot an outlaw had in cash, gold or treasure, they could find sanctuary and freedom from the worry a back-shooter might surprise them in the night.

Daughter had a sheriff and two deputies, but as long as a man minded his own business, didn't cheat when he gambled and avoided public drunkenness, they didn't bother them about any wanted posters that might be floating around.

In fact, it was the sheriff's job to collect the ten percent levy from any outlaw riding into town and turn it over to the mayor and town council, who pocketed most of it.

Of the six hundred residents living in Daughtry, it was estimated that ten percent were wanted by the law. It was never asked why by the townspeople if they could afford the levy. Some outlaws came and went on a regular basis, using Daughtry as a place to rest up between jobs. Some made it their home and only left when they needed money and returned when they had it.

When Dix rode into town, he stopped by the sheriff's office to let him know he wasn't wanted anywhere and just wanted a few peaceful days to rest up before heading south into Mexico.

The sheriff had a thousand wanted posters from across the country. Dix wasn't on any of them.

Dix was a tall man, several inches over six feet and built lean and hard. His hair and eyes were dark, his face hard angles that spoke of a man who had seen much and didn't like most of what he saw.

He kept to himself, didn't enter a saloon or brothel and spent a great deal of his time in a chair on the porch with a cup of coffee and a newspaper and a cigarette.

In the afternoon on the third day in town, Dix was reading a newspaper and drinking coffee on the porch of the hotel when three men rode into town and dismounted across the street at the saloon.

They entered the saloon and Dix stood up, went into the hotel to his room. He went through his saddlebags for the wanted poster on the three men, the McCall brothers, Tom, Tim and Mario. Their father was Irish, but their mother was Mexican and sometimes Mario, the youngest of the three was called Little Mary.

Dix folded the wanted poster and stuck it into his shirt pocket. Then he removed the warrant from the saddlebags and tucked it away with the poster.

Dix removed his holster from the coat hook on the wall and strapped it on. He checked his Colt Peacemaker to make sure it was fully loaded. The Colt was chambered for .45 Long ammunition. The sights were custom made, the trigger honed to a hair's touch and the grips made of black ivory with a gold cross on the left side of the grip.

Dix left his room, went down to the lobby and got a fresh cup of coffee from the cantina and took it across the street. He sat in a chair outside the saloon and rolled a cigarette from his pouch and papers.

Thirty minutes later, after the McCall brothers had a few drinks, they appeared again on the sidewalk. They started for their horses when Dix stood up and approached them from behind.

"That's it, boys," Dix said. "Don't move."

"Who's that?" Tom said.

"Turn around slow," Dix said. "I shoot no man in the back."

Tom, Tim and Mario turned and faced Dix.

"Each of you men is worth two hundred dollars," Dix said. "Dead or alive. I prefer alive, but it's up to you."

"Are you crazy, mister?" Tom said. "This is Daughtry. You can't arrest a man in Daughtry."

"I've watched you since you rode in," Dix said. "You haven't been to the sheriff yet to pay for your sanctuary."

"We was just about to," Tom said.

"About to isn't good enough," Dix said. "About to means you didn't."

"Three of us, Tom," Tim said. "Let's just shoot this asshole."

"I'd prefer you didn't," Dix said. "You're young men. Serve your ten years and you'll still be young men. The alternative is you die as young men."

"What's alternative mean?" Mario said.

"It means you drop your guns and come with me to see the sheriff," Dix said.

"Screw you," Mario said.

"You don't have to be rude about it," Dix said.

"I'll give you rude, you sum bitch," Mario said.

"No, don't," Tom yelled.

Mario reached for his pistol and Dix drew his Colt and shot him dead. That forced Tom and Tim to draw their pistols and the outcome of that was Dix shot them dead as well.

A crowd gathered around Dix and the three dead McCall brothers. The sheriff and his two deputies pushed through the crowd. They carried shotguns and aimed them at Dix.

"You can't shoot people in Daughtry," the sheriff said. "It's against the rules of the town council."

Dix removed the wanted poster from his pocket and handed it to the sheriff. "The McCall brothers," he said. "Wanted dead or alive. The bounty is six hundred dollars."

"Are you a bounty hunter?" the sheriff said. "We don't allow them in Daughtry. If word got out we allowed bounty hunters, we'd be out of business."

Dix removed the warrant from his pocket and his badge from another pocket. "My name is Dix and I'm a dully sworn Federal

Warrant Officer of the federal court," he said. "The warrant is issued by a federal judge, sheriff. It's all nice and legal."

The sheriff looked at Dix.

"These three didn't stop by and see you to pay their fee for protection when the unfortunate incident occurred, so technically I didn't violate your rule."

"You expect me to pay you six hundred dollars?" the sheriff said.

"No, I expect you to write a sworn affidavit that the McCall brothers are dead, killed by my hand," Dix said. "I'll pick it up on my way out of town."

Dix walked away from the crowd and entered the hotel.

The sheriff looked at the McCall brothers. "Somebody get these poor bastards off the street," he said.

About an hour later, Dix rode his horse to the sheriff's office, dismounted and entered the office where the sheriff was at his desk.

"You come for your statement?" the sheriff said and picked up a document from his desk and handed it to Dix.

"Thank you," Dix said.

"The town isn't happy about this," the sheriff said.

Dix scanned the document, then folded it

and put it into a pocket. “They’ll get over it,” he said. “Have a good day, sheriff.”

Chapter Two

As he sat beside a campfire and ate a supper of beans, bacon, cornbread and coffee, Dix reviewed his paperwork.

He left Washington DC four months ago with twelve warrants issued by federal judge Alan Pickford. Just one remained to be served. Of the eleven, just two chose prison over death.

The twelfth warrant was on a man wanted for cattle theft in New Mexico. He was hiding out in El Paso. The bounty was one thousand dollars, offered by the Stock Growers Association of New Mexico.

The twelve warrants added up to fifteen thousand dollars. He would collect the money upon returning to Washington to see Judge Pickford.

Dix came out of the war fourteen years ago without a trade or a home. His Indiana farm had been burned and his parents murdered by rebel raiders in sixty-four and there was no reason to return to a worn out patch of land and cinders of a house.

He was part of a sniper squad attached to Sherman and he stopped counting the number of men he killed after the number reached fifty. After Lee's surrender, Dix stayed with the army another year to provide security to the South at the start of reconstruction.

When he was discharged, his only skill was with a gun. Grant needed men to work for the railroad as police officers for the Transcontinental Railroad project. Faced with no job, money or future back in Indiana, Dix went to work as a railroad police officer, a federal job that paid fifty dollars a month to start. Grant appointed him the rank of First Lieutenant.

Dix was part of just twenty-four men assigned as railroad police. He kept his rank of Lieutenant for the next four years.. The job of the railroad police was protection and security against Indians, outlaws, thieves and, on occasion, each other. The railroad created towns along the way and with towns came saloons and prostitutes and gambling and fights were an everyday occurrence, especially over women.

During the winter months, operations shut down and workers went home, but not the police. They stayed behind and lived on the trains until spring and the workers returned and work resumed.

By the time the job was completed on May 10th, 1869, Dix had a pay of seventy-five-dollars a month and saved most of it.

By then, Dix had enough of the army and returned to Indiana. The place where the house once stood was an overgrown empty hole. Same for the barn. The two hundred acres he and his father plowed and planted corn and potatoes hadn't be touched for going on seven years.

Dix paid the taxes out of his pay, so the property was still his, but he didn't want it. He went to town and sold the property for twelve hundred dollars and was done with it. He put the money in the Wells Fargo bank in Fort Wayne and started drifting.

He worked as a cowboy for a ranch in Kansas for a year for thirty a month, but he couldn't save much.

From there he tried working a claim in Colorado. After eighteen months, he pulled in just a thousand dollars.

In 1873, he took a job as a deputy sheriff in Denver, a goldrush town of about five thousand people. The pay was a hundred a month, plus meals and ammunition. There he met Victoria, the daughter of a general store owner. A year later, they married. A month after the wedding, while Dix was transporting a prisoner to Cheyenne, Wyoming, six men rode in and robbed the Wells Fargo Bank, killing the sheriff and two other deputies in the process.

Directly across the street from the bank was the general store where Victoria worked. A stray bullet entered the store through the front window and struck her in the head, killing her instantly.

When Dix returned from Cheyenne, the outraged town wanted to make him sheriff and for him to track the men down and bring them to justice.

Dix saw the county judge, a man named Alan Pickford, who issued six John Doe warrants for the bank robbers.

He took the warrants and left the badge. For the next eighteen months, he hunted the six men who robbed the bank and murdered his wife. The men split up shortly after the robbery, but the money they stole was railroad payroll money and the serial numbers were logged and distributed to banks across the country.

Through telegrams, Dix kept in touch with the judge and every time the stolen money was spent and recorded, the judge was able to notify Dix of the locations.

By seventy-five, Dix found and killed all six of the men. When he returned to Denver, he discovered that Pickford had become a federal judge with a position in Washington.

Dix traveled to Washington to return the six warrants to Pickford. Wells Fargo had offered a reward of ten thousand dollars for the six men, but since Dix had never actually resigned his position, he was ineligible to collect the money.

"I didn't do it for the money, Judge," Dix told him. "I did it for my wife."

Pickford had a bottle of whiskey in his chambers. He poured two drinks and handed one to Dix. "So what are your plans?" he said. "I don't have any," Dix said.

"A man has got to have plans, Dix," Pickford said. "It's what separate us from the animals. An animal is incapable of planning his future. Only a human can do that."

"Maybe so, but at the moment, I'm just going to drift for a while and see the country," Dix said.

"I've looked at your record carefully, Dix," Pickford said. "Excellent war record, four years with the railroad as a police officer with the rank of lieutenant. Deputy sheriff in Denver. I would like to swear you in."

"As what?" Dix said.

"A dully sworn Federal Warrant Officer,"

Pickford said.

"Warrant Officer?" Dix said.

"A sheriff's authority is limited to a town or a county," Pickford said. "A marshal is federal and responsible for keeping the peace in a territory. None have the resources or the time to chase down every outlaw with a price on his head. A warrant officer, however, that's all he does is serve warrants. Your income is determined by how many warrants you serve to a successful conclusion."

"I'm going to drift for a while, judge," Dix said. "But I'll keep your offer in mind just in case I happen to formulate a plan."

For the next fourteen months, Dix drifted west to Kansas, Nebraska, Montana Territory, the Dakotas, Arizona and Wyoming. He drew on his account with Wells Fargo when money ran short. Other times he took odd jobs, anything from cowboying to clerking in a store to build up a small stake and then he would ride off again.

Along the way, Dix saw many different Indian tribes, traded with some of them and made friends with others.

Mostly he kept to himself as he drifted. Sometimes he thought about the farm back in Indians. If not for the war, would he still be there, plowing fields with his father?

Probably.

If not for the six outlaws that robbed the bank and murdered his wife, would he have children by now?

Probably.

Pickford was right in one regard, that only humans can make plans. Animals run on instinct alone. They do what nature programed them to do. Humans are the only creature on earth that can really make plans for their lives.

However, as most people discover, most of the plans they make never work out. Animals, unlike people are spared the heartache of plans that don't work out. Of failed farms and businesses, of wives that died forty years too soon, of the horrors of war and seeing the misery one man can cause another.

One night, as he spread out in his bedroll beside a campfire and watched the stars, he thought about this beaver that lived in the creek by the farmhouse in Indiana when he was a boy. The beaver would build a dam in the creek and his father would always destroy it. Operating on instinct, the beaver would rebuild the dam and his father would again destroy it. The beaver didn't know heartache over his destroyed dam as he went strictly by instinct, whereas humans would suffer over their home being destroyed.

The beaver simply went about his business and rebuilt the dam.

Riding through Wyoming, Dix camped along the Snake River for a week. He fished and hunted and saw buffalo and herds of wild horses. He saw passing Indians from a reservation on a hunting party. Open ranges of tall grass where cattle could grow fat and a man could make a living in the open air and free country.

He rode to Cheyenne to the land office. Land was plentiful if a man wanted to start a cattle ranch, if he had the money.

Ten thousand acres was the recommended amount of land to start, preferable by a creek or river. Then a house, barn, coral and bunkhouse and several hundred head of cattle and a bull to start.

At two dollars an acre, just the land would cost twenty thousand dollars. To start a ranch, he needed fifty thousand minimum, taking into account contingency money to get through the first winter.

A ranch was a rich man's dream.

Dix left Cheyenne and drifted for a bit and one night as he sat by a campfire and at a supper of beans and bacon, he remembered Judge Pickford's office.

Chapter Three

Dix sat across the table from Judge Pickford in a Washington DC restaurant and sipped from his glass of Irish whiskey.

"Stop by my chambers in the morning and I'll have your money and some new warrants," Pickford said.

"Thank you, Judge," Dix said.

"Still have a cattle ranch in mind?" Pickford said.

"I'm a ways off, but yeah."

"How much do you have squirreled away?"

"Twenty thousand and a bit," Dix said.

"It might take another two years," Pickford said.

"I figured," Dix said.

"You could try to start now," Pickford said.

"No, I want to do it right," Dix said. Or not at all."

"Well, stop by my chambers in the morning," Pickford said.

After leaving the judge, Dix walked around for a bit. The night air was heavy with heat, making it impossible to sleep, so he went into a large saloon for a cold beer.

He wasn't armed. Public wearing's of firearms was prohibited in Washington, but he had a Derringer in his pocket and he would bet that every man in the saloon had the same.

Dix ordered a beer and found a small table against a wall. He rolled a cigarette and lit it with a wood match. On the balcony of the saloon, six sporting women looked down on the crowd.

A pretty blonde with gray eyes caught his attention and she smiled at him. She came down the stairs and went to his table. "Buy a girl a drink?" she said.

"Have a seat," Dix said.

She sat. "My name is Trixie," she said.

"Dix."

"You look sad."

"Do I?"

"For a two-dollar bottle and five dollars, I can make you happy," Trixie said.

"Upstairs?" Dix said.

"I'm no alley cat," Trixie said.

"I have a room," Dix said.

"That's extra if I have to leave the saloon."

"The Eden Rock, room 212," Dix said. "I want to take a bath. Give me an hour."

"I brought a bottle," Trixie said when Dix opened the door to his hotel room.

Dix was wearing just a robe after taking a bath. "Fix us a drink," he said.

There were two water glasses and a pitcher of water on the dresser. While Trixie poured two drinks, Dix sat in a chair and rolled a cigarette.

Trixie brought Dix a glass and kept one for herself as she sat on the bed. "Don't bother to get dressed," she said. "But I do have to ask you for the seven dollars in advance."

Dix reached for his pants on the bed and removed two twenty-dollar gold pieces from a pocket and handed them to Trixie. "Will this cover until morning?" he said.

"Mister, this covers the entire week," Trixie said as she stood and opened her blouse.

Dix ordered room service for breakfast and he and Trixie ate at the table beside the window

"I've never had a man pamper me so," Trixie said. "I almost feel guilty taking your money."

Sipping coffee, Dix looked at her over the rim of his cup.

"I said almost," Trixie said.

"Well, I have to get going," Dix said.

"Will you be back?" Trixie said.

"Yes, but I can't say when."

"Look me up when you do."

"I'll do that," Dix said.

"I have nine federal warrants here, Dix," Pickford said. "All nine wanted for murder. Some for robbery as well."

Dix picked up the warrants and put them into his jacket pocket.

"Here is a bank draft for fifteen thousand, four hundred dollars for the last bunch and five hundred in expense money," Pickford said. "Those nine warrants add up to eleven thousand and five hundred dollars. Get them all and you're that much closer to your ranch."

"I'll see you in a few months, Judge," Dix said.

Dix sat at the table in his hotel room with a cup of coffee and smoked a rolled cigarette. He read each warrant and arranged them by location. Closest to Washington was Billy Cass, a twenty-nine-year-old small-time stage coach robber who moved up the ladder when he shot and killed the shotgunner during his last robbery. The stage coach was traveling from Conway, Arkansas to Little Rock when Cass held it up, using a shotgun.

The shotgunner attempted to shoot Cass, but Cass beat him to the trigger and nearly cut the man in half with two barrels of twelve gage. Cass escaped with about a thousand dollars from the passengers and twelve-thousand from the cash box riding up top with the luggage. That money was bound for the Bank of Little Rock and it was the bank and the Overland Stage Coach Company that posted a two-thousand-dollar reward for his capture, dead or alive.

Cass was last seen riding into the Indian Nation west of Fort Smith.

Dix caught an afternoon train to Fort Smith. The Indian Nation was in the Ozark Mountains and the mountains spilled over into Oklahoma. It wasn't going to be easy locating Cass in the mountains. Since the robbery two months ago, he's had ample time to set up camp and wait out the law.

The train arrived in Fort Smith at nine o'clock in the evening. Dx checked into the Hotel Fort Smith, had his horse stabled and grabbed a bite to eat at the hotel restaurant and then went directly to bed.

His plan was to get an early start in the morning.

Chapter Four

After breakfast, Dix purchased a forty-dollar mule at the livery. At the general store, he purchased one dozen blankets, four boxes of Winchester ammunition, six hunting knives, a dozen sacks of coffee, six sacks of sugar and a dozen bags of jerked beef.

For himself, he purchased ten days' worth of supplies.

Then he headed west into the mountains.

He expected to see nothing the first day. He made camp at night and got an early start the next morning. By mid-day, he was in the Nation where the five civilized tribes ruled the day.

He knew he was being watched. By which tribe and how many was a guess. He stopped, made camp, built a fire and put on some beans and bacon to cook and a pot of coffee.

After the coffee boiled, he filled a cup and rolled a cigarette. He rested his back against the saddle and waited.

Six Cherokee warriors riding bareback rode into his camp and looked at him. They had two elk slung over two horses. One spoke to him in English.

"You are not allowed here according to the treaty," he said.

Dix took out his badge and pinned it to his shirt. "I am a lawman and I seek your help," he said.

The one who spoke dismounted and walked to Dix. "I am called Waya," he said.

"The Wolf," Dix said. "A good strong name."

"You speak Cherokee," Waya said.

"Some. Would you care for some coffee?" Dix said.

Waya sat opposite Dix. Dix filled a second cup and gave it to Waya.

"What help do you seek?" Waya said.

"I am after a white man wanted for murder," Dix said. "He left Fort Smith and went into the mountains about one month ago. He probably plans to wait until the law gives up looking for him before he comes down."

Waya sipped his coffee.

"I don't come emptyhanded," Dix said. "That mule and everything on it is a gift for you out of respect."

"We know where this man went," Waya

said. "And we accept you gift of kindness."

Waya turned and spoke to his men in Cherokee. One rode to the mule, took its reins and then he and the other four rode away.

"I will take you to him," Waya said. "A day's ride from here."

"Care for some lunch?' Dix said. "The store bought biscuits are pretty good."

Dix and Waya rode west high into the mountains until, by nightfall they camped in a canyon near a stream.

They built a fire. Dix cooked a supper of fresh beef stew with crusty bread and coffee. They tended to the horses until the coffee was ready and they sat beside the fire to drink a cup.

Dix rolled a cigarette.

"How much longer?" Dix said.

"Tomorrow when the sun is directly overhead, we will be there," Waya said.

"Is it Oklahoma Territory?" Dix said.

"Yes, in what you call Oklahoma," Waya said.

The stew was ready and Dix filled two bowls and passed one to Waya. "Grab a hunk of bread," he said.

The mountains didn't hold the heat of the day and they built up the fire and placed their bedrolls beside it and fell asleep watching the stars. They weren't white and Indian. They were just two men watching the stars.

Noon the following day, Dix and Ways crawled to the top of a hill and looked down on a cabin, corral and small barn. Smoke rose up from the chimney. Four horses were in the corral.

Three men and a woman were seated in chairs on the porch and they were pulling on a jig of corn liquor.

"Who's who?" Dix said.

"The big Cherokee on the end is Blue Duck," Waya said.

"The outlaw?"

"Yes. The skinny one next to the woman is Sam Starr," Waya said. "The woman is his wife, Belle Starr. The fourth one beside Belle is the man you hunt."

Dix took out the wanted poster and looked at it, then used his binoculars to zoom in on the man's face. "That's Cass alright," he said.

"Let me see," Waya said.

Dix handed the binoculars to Waya, who looked through them and was shocked.

"You like them?" Dix said.

"Very much."

"Keep them and use them for hunting,"

Dix said. "I have another pair."

They stood and walked back to their horses. "Well, I best go down and get him," Dix said.

"Alone?" Waya said.

"I thank you for guiding me and enjoy the binoculars," Dix said. He opened his saddlebags and removed a spare Colt and stuck it in his belt, then mounted the saddle.

Then he rode down the hill toward the cabin. He covered the distance of three-hundred-yards in a matter of a few minutes. As he neared the cabin, Cass jumped off the porch and ran around to the rear.

Dix reached the cabin, dismounted and walked up to the porch.

"You be the law," Belle said.

"Course he's the law," Sam Starr said. "Don't you see that badge there on his shirt?"

Blue Duck stood up and pulled a large knife. Dix drew his Colt and smacked Blue Duck in the head and he fell unconscious to the porch floor.

Belle and Sam looked at Blue Duck.

"Tell him when he wakes up, I'm after that skinny fellow who jumped off the porch and no hard feelings," Dix said.

"You ain't after us?" Belle said.

"If I was, you would know about it," Dix said.

"I expect we would," Belle said.

"Did he pay you to hide him out?" Dix said.

"Five double eagles," Belle said.

"I'll give you the like amount if you saddle his horse for me," Dix said.

Belle nodded.

Dix reached into his pocket and counted out one hundred dollars in bills and gave them to Belle. "Be back directly," he said.

Dix returned to his horse, mounted the saddle and road around to the side of the cabin. Directly ahead, three hundred yards, Cass was running. Dix didn't hurry. Cass was faltering badly.

Dix said, "Let's go, boy," and sped up a bit and closed the gap to a hundred feet.

Cass herd him coming, turned and grabbed his pistol and stared firing wildly.

Dix and his horse, ignored the shots and kept riding. Cass tossed his empty gun away and tried to run faster, but he was exhausted and dizzy and started running in circles.

Dix grabbed his lasso from the saddle loop, swung it overhead and roped Cass around the waist and Cass fell to the ground.

Dix dismounted and walked to Cass. On

all fours, Cass vomited into the grass, then rolled over onto his back.

"If you're done losing your lunch, let's go," Dix said.

"I can't," Cass gasped. "I'm too tired."

"Then I'll drag you in back of my horse," Dix said.

"You don't give a man no room," Cass said.

"About as much as you gave the poor bastard you blew in half with your shotgun," Dix said. "Get up. Let's go."

Belle and Sam Starr were still pulling on the jug of corn liquor when Dix returned with Cass roped behind the horse.

Cass's horse was saddle and hitched to the porch railing.

"Bule Duck is feeling poorly from the bump you have him on the head," Belle said. "He went in to sleep it off."

"Tell him I meant no offense," Dix said. "Cass, get on your horse."

When Dix and Cass reached the top of the hill that lead to a pass, Waya was waiting for them.

"Why, that's a stinking savage," Cass said.

"Shut up," Dix said. "I thought you left," he said to Waya.

"I wanted to see what would happen,"

Ways said.

"A stinking, no good, savage," Cass said.

"Cass, I tell you to shut up again, you'll ride the whole way back bound and gagged," Dix said.

"If you want, I'll scalp him for you," Waya said.

"Keep that stinking heathen away from me," Cass yelled.

"Waya, lead the way," Dix said.

Two days later, after a hot breakfast, Dix and Waya parted ways. Dix extended his right hand. "My people have a custom when parting ways to shake hands," Dix said.

"Come again," Ways said as he shook Dix's hand. "We can always use another good mule."

Chapter Five

Judge Isaac Parker was appointed territorial judge by President Grant four years ago in seventy-five to bring the law to a lawless Arkansas.

By appointing thirty U.S. Marshals and taking a stern approach from the beach, Fort Smith and Arkansas slowly became civilized.

Dix stood in Parker's chambers while Parker sat behind his desk and read the warrant on Cass.

"He's in the holding jail?" Parker said.

"As of fifteen minutes ago," Dix said.

Parker returned the warrant to Dix. "I know Judge Pickford," he said. "He's a good man. Give him my regards next time you see him."

"I will. About Cass?" Dix said.

"He'll be tried," Parker said. "And hung."

"I'll be at the Hotel if you need me," Dix

said. "Until the noon train tomorrow."

Dix had a shave and a bath at the barber shop, then dropped off his dirty clothes at the Chinese laundry and then went for a steak.

Alone at a table in a restaurant, Dix studied the remaining warrants and decided to go after the Olson brothers. Three brothers, they specialized in robbing banks in small towns, Bob Olson was the oldest at twenty-nine, James was next at twenty-seven and Billy the youngest at just twenty.

Small towns tended to have just one sheriff and most of them were part time and unwilling to risk their neck for just a few dollars. Since the most they ever got from a bank was twelve-hundred-dollars, the brothers had to stay active and rob a lot of banks.

All told, they robbed twenty-three banks before anyone even knew who they were. Their downfall came when they robbed the bank in their hometown of Helena, Montana.

Even though they always covered their faces with bandanas and wore their hats over their eyes, the teller recognized their voices and called them out by name.

Helena was a small town of just three

thousand people, but on that day, fate played a hand in the outcome. A U.S. Marshal happened to be in town and in fact, in the bank when they attempted to rob it.

A shootout occurred. The marshal was wounded. The bank teller was wounded. James Olson was wounded. The Olson brothers got away without a dime, but they got away.

Cowboys by trade, the brothers went on the run and weren't seen for close to a year until a cowboy from Helena recognized them working on a ranch in Nebraska near Ogallala.

The railroad didn't stop in Ogallala, so he would have to ride from the North Platte to find them.

The next day, before catching the noon train, Dix stopped by to see Judge Parker in his chambers.

"Where are you off to?" Parker said.

"Nebraska to pick up three bank robbers," Dix said.

"Good luck," Parker said.

"Thanks, Judge," Dix said. "If I get back this way, I stop in and say hello."

CHAPTER SIX

After two days in the saddle, Dix reached the Jensen Ranch, a medium size ranch north of Ogallala.

He reached the ranch shortly before sunset. A man of about fifty and a woman of about twenty sat in chairs on the porch, both with cups of coffee.

"Evening," Dix said. :My name is Dix. I'm a Federal Warrant Officer. Would you be Mr. Jensen?"

Jensen looked at the badge pinned to Dix's shirt. "I am. This is my daughter Kate," he said.

"May I step down and have a word with you?" Dix said.

"You may. Kate, get some coffee for Mr. Dix," Jensen said.

Kate went into the house and returned with a cup before Dix could claim a chair on the porch.

"Thank you, ma'am," Dix said as he took

the cup from Kate.

"Now how can I help you?" Jensen said.

"I'm looking for a man name Kelly," Dix said. "First name is Kevin. I understand he works here."

"What's he done the law wants him?" Jensen said.

"Nothing," Dix said. "I have warrants for three bank robbers. Kelly recognized them from his home town and notified the law he knows where they are hiding. I want to speak to him about that."

"Kate, set a plate at the table for Mr. Dix," Jensen said. "Mr. Dix, the men are having supper. It can wait until then. In the meantime, my daughter is a hell of a cook."

And she was. She served beef stew with carrots and potatoes and fresh, crusty bread with apple pie for dessert with a whipped cream topping. Kate used a hand-crank, egg beater to whip the heavy cream into fluffy peaks.

"That was an elegant dinner, Kate," Dix said.

"Thank you," Kate said.

"Kate, we'll be at the bunkhouse," Jensen said.

Jensen walked Dix the two hundred yards to the bunkhouse where his six hands were playing cards at a table.

"Excuse me, boys," Jensen said. "Keven, may we have a quick word with you, son?"

Kyle stood up from the table and walked to Jensen. "Yes sir?" he said.

"Outside," Jensen said.

Jensen, Dix and Kelly went outside and Jensen closed the door.

"This is Mr. Dix. He is a Federal Warrant Officer," Jensen said.

"You know where the Olson brothers are hiding," Dix said. "You contacted the Justice Department by mail, claiming you know where they are. Is that correct?"

"The reward for information is still there, isn't it?" Kelly said.

"Yes," Dix said.

"The doctor in Montana says if I don't get my ma to Arizona she will die of consumption," Kelly said. "I've been saving to move the family, but it's hard on thirty dollars a month."

"Keven, why didn't you ever mention that to me?" Jensen said. "I could advance you the money."

"And work for years to pay you back? I'll never get to see my ma that way," Kelly said.

"You'll get the one thousand dollars," Dix said. "If the Olson brothers are where you claim."

"They are," Kelly said. "I went to town to

pick up wire and a few other supplies and I saw them in the general store with Mr. Frazier. I was shocked to see them because I knew from back home they was bad men."

"Did you know they were wanted at the time?" Dix said.

"I didn't know until weeks later when Mr. Jensen sent me to town to mail some letters for him and pick up the mail. There was a reward poster in the post office. I took it down and wrote to the Justice Department like it said."

"That was months ago," Dix said.

"I know, but they're still there," Kelly said. "On Saturday's I ride over to Mr. Frazier's, hide and check with binoculars. They were there as of five days ago."

"Okay, Keven. You did your part," Dix said. "I'll handle the rest."

"Thanks, Keven," Jensen said. "Go back to your game now."

Dix and Jensen walked back to the house.

"Fool kid never said a word about his mother," Jensen said.

"At his age, would you?" Dix said.

"I expect not," Jensen said.

"How many men does Frazier employ?" Dix said.

"Six, same as me."

"Where can I find the Frazier Ranch?"

Dix said.

"Ten miles southwest, but you'll never find it after dark," Jensen said. "Stay the night and get a fresh start in the morning."

"Is there room in the bunkhouse?" Dix said.

"Nonsense," Jensen said. "I have three extra bedrooms. My wife and son passed ten years ago. It's just me and Kate now. You got your pick of any of the three."

"Alright, I'll take you up on your offer," Dix said.

"Kate serves breakfast at eight o'clock," Jensen said. "Don't be late. Her breakfast is as good as her supper."

CHAPTER SEVEN

"That was a wonderful breakfast, Kate. Thank you," Dix said on the porch.

Kate smiled. "You're welcome," she said.

"I'll walk you to the corral," Jensen said.

They left the porch and walked to the corral where Dix saddled his horse.

"How do you plan to take three men to trial?" Jensen said.

"Peacefully, I hope," Dix said.

"If they resist?"

Dix mounted the saddle and looked at Jensen. "You'll hear about it, I expect," he said. "Thanks for your hospitality."

Dix rode southwest for about ten miles until he reached an open range where cows were grazing.

He rode another mile and came to another range where three cowboys were working on branding cows.

One man did the branding, two men roped and brought the cows to the ground.

The other three herded cows to the fire.

Dix rode to the fire. The man with the branding iron looked at him, then at his badge.

"You'll be Bob," Dix said. "Which is James and Billy."

"We ain't armed," Bob said.

"Then I have no reason to shoot you," Dix said.

James and Billy rode up behind Bob and dismounted. "What is it, Bob?" James said.

"Law's caught up with us," Bob said.

"There's three of us, Bob," Billy said. "We can take him."

"Make one move and I will kill the three of you where you stand," Dix said.

"He means it, Billy," Bob said.

"Better believe I mean it," Dix said. "Now, you have some choices to make. The first is you put up a fight and you ride back draped over the saddle and then be buried in some potter's field. Two, you come peacefully, don't resist and serve your time. You never killed anybody and you'll probably get seven years. That's a long time, but you'll still be young men and can start over when you get out."

Bob looked at James and Billy. "Boys?" he said.

"In a way, I'm glad it's over," James said.

"I guess I can do my time," Billy said.

"Let's ride over and see Mr. Frazier and I'll explain things to him," Dix said.

While Bob, James and Billy packed their gear in the bunkhouse, Dix spoke with Frazier on the porch of the house.

"The darndest thing is that those boys are damn good cowboys," Frazier said.

Bob, James and Billy rode their horses to the house. "We're ready," Bob said.

"Boys, do your time, keep your nose clean and when you get out, you'll have jobs waiting for you," Frazier said.

"Thank you, sir," Bob said. "We appreciate it and we'll be back."

"Ain't you going to tie us up or something?" Bob said when they made camp for the evening.

"No," Dix said. "Get a fire going. Mr. Frazier gave us some decent steaks."

After building a fire, Dix put on a pan of beans, a pot of coffee and then cooked four steaks in the large fry pan.

"So what happened in Helena?" Dix said as they ate.

"Oh, that bank teller," Bob said. "He took a shot at us and hit the marshal in the leg. The marshal shot the teller as he fell down and the teller shot James in the shoulder as he hit the floor."

Dix laughed. "So you didn't shoot anybody?"

"We never shot anybody in our life," Bob said.

"Hell, boys, you might get only five years," Dix said.

"Mr. Dix, what kind of lawman are you anyway?" Billy said. "You don't tie us up, you feed us like we was at a hotel, I don't get it."

"I'm a dully sworn, Federal Warrant Officer," Dix said. "I treat men by the way the act. If you act like a man, you get treated like one. That's all there is to it. That's all there ever was to it."

"You'll get no trouble from us," Bob said.

"Good," Dix said. "Because I could really use some sleep."

Dix turned the Olson brothers over to the court in Helena, Montana.

"Mr. Dix, you treated us fair," Bob said.

"Boys, do your time like men, keep your nose clean and you'll be free before you know it," Dix said.

They shook hands.

"So long, boys," Dix said.

Chapter Eight

Dix handed Judge Pickford the nine warrants. "Pour us a drink," Pickford said.

Dix went to the bar in the corner of Pickford's chambers and filled two shot glasses with whiskey and gave one to Pickford.

"You must be getting close to your ranch by now," Pickford said.

"After you cut me a draft tomorrow, I'll have thirty thousand in the bank," Dix said. "I need another year's work, maybe two."

"There's no shortage of work, believe me," Pickford said.

"I'll see you tomorrow," Dix said. "I'm going to get cleaned up and grab a steak."

"Nice to see you again, Mr. Dix," the clerk at the Eden Rock Hotel said. "Shave and a bath?"

"I could use a steak, too," Dix said. "Bath first."

Dix shaved before getting into the tub,

then afterward dressed in clean clothing and dropped off his laundry at the desk.

About to enter the hotel restaurant, he changed his mind and left the hotel. He walked to the saloon where Trixie worked, entered and went to the bar. "A shot of whiskey, please," he told the bartender.

The bartender poured a shot and Dix left fifty cents on the bar. Holding the shot glass, Dix walked up the stairs to where the ladies waited.

"What's your pleasure, mister?" one of the women said.

"Trixie," Dix said.

"I'm afraid Trixie is unavailable," the woman said.

"If she's with somebody, I can wait," Dix said.

"No, she's just unavailable," the woman said.

"Tell her Dix was asking for her," Dix said. He turned and was about to walk down the steps when a door opened and Trixie said, "Come in."

Dix entered the room and Trixie closed the door. The shades were drawn and the room was dark.

"Can you light a lamp?" Dix said.

"No."

"Why not?"

"I don't want you to see me," Trixie said.

Dix set the shot glass on a table and struck a match, then lit a lantern on the same table. He looked at Trixie. Her face was bruised, she had a black eye and her lower lip was swollen.

"What happened?" Dix said.

"I fell."

"That's a fist mark on your face," Dix said.

"It's not the first time I've been hit," Trixie said.

"Who did it?" Dix said.

"It doesn't matter," Trixie said.

"It does to me."

"Why. I'm nothing but a common whore to you," Trixie said.

"Do you remember the hotel I stayed at?" Dix said.

"Yes."

"I'm in the same room. Meet me there later tonight."

"I can't go out looking like this."

"Wear a vail."

Dix left the room and closed the door. The women were still on the balcony. "Who did that?" Dix said.

The women stared at him.

"I won't ask again," Dix said.

"A little shitbird named Congressman

Markus Post," one of the women said.

"A congressman?" Dix said.

"He likes to hit women," the woman said.

"Where can I find him?" Dix said.

"Mister, we don't want no . . ." the woman said.

"Where?" Dix said.

A woman in back stepped forward. "I know," she said. "I'll take you there. The son of a bitch beat me up once. I never forgot it."

"Let's go."

"Let me get my wrap."

Dix and the woman walked along a side street. It was after dark and street lanterns illuminated the way.

"What he does is he invites a girl to his house with the promise of a hundred dollars, then he beats the tar out of her," the woman said. "Then he pays the hundred and puts her in a taxi."

"Why would Trixie go with him?" Dix said.

"She didn't know. By the time she found out it was too late."

"And you never call the police?"

"On a congressman?"

She stopped in front of a nice brownstone building. "This is it," she said.

Dix looked up at the two-story building. Lanterns shone in several windows on the first floor.

"He's home," Dix said.

"Appears so."

"Go knock on the door," Dix said. "Tell him you're here for your date."

"I don't want to get beat up again."

"You won't," Dix said.

Dix and the woman walked up the steps to the front door. "Knock," Dix said as he stood aside.

The woman knocked on the door. "Congressman Post, it's Angel, I'm here for our date," she said.

The door opened. Post, dressed in a silk robe, looked at her. "I don't recall having a date," he said.

"I could swear you said tonight," Angel said. "Well, another time then."

"No, wait, as long as you're here," Post said.

Dix pushed past Angel and punched Post in the face, knocking him to the floor. Dix entered the house, followed by Angel, who closed the door.

Bleeding, Post looked up at Dix.

"You can't do this," Post said. "I'm a sitting congressman."

Dix grabbed Post and yanked him to his

feet. Then he punched him several more times, threw him to the floor and kicked him in the ribs and stomach.

"Hit another woman and you'll never walk again," Dix said. "Congressman."

Dix turned to the door and Angel was staring at him with a strange, little smile on her face.

CHAPTER NINE

Dix opened the door when Trixie knocked. She wore a full-length jacket and a hat with a dark, fishnet vail.

"Come in," Dix said.

Trixie entered and he closed the door.

"I don't know why I bothered to come here," she said as she removed the hat and jacket. "I can't service you right now. I'm a bit torn up and so sore I could hardly get dressed."

"Do you know what's the best thing for soreness? A hot bath," Dix said. "I reserved the bathing room so you won't be disturbed."

"You're kidding?"

"I'm not," Dix said. "Come on."

As Trixie soaked in a tub full of hot water and salts, Dix sat in a chair and read a newspaper. He had a cup of coffee and rolled a cigarette.

"Why?" Trixie said.

Dix looked up. "Why what?"

"Angel told me what you did and now this bath, why?"

"No reason," Dix said.

"You beat up a congressman and paid at least twenty-dollars to reserve this private bath for no reason," Trixie said. "I can't even service you the shape I'm in."

"How's that water?" Dix said.

"Cooling off."

Dix stood and went to the woodstove where several buckets of water were heating up. He grabbed a bucket and brought it to the tub and poured the water into the tub by Trixie's ankles.

"Better?" he said.

"Yes."

"Meet me back in the room in twenty-minutes," Dix said.

"Where are you going?"

"Twenty minutes."

Room service brought a dinner of baked chicken with vegetables, pie for dessert, coffee and a bottle of red wine.

As they ate dinner, Trixie said, "What do you do? For a living, I mean."

Dix stood up and went to his jacket hanging on the coat hook and returned with his badge and handed it to Trixie. "Federal Warrant Officer," she said. "Is that like a sheriff or marshal?"

"Similar," Dix said. "My job is to issue federal warrants to outlaws, to arrest them and bring them in for trial."

"I see," Trixie said. "So you hunt outlaws?"

"You're simplifying it, but that's the general gist of it," Dix said. "How's the soreness?"

"A little better," Trixie said. "I still can't . . ."

"I'm not asking you to," Dix said.

"I can send over Angel, she was most impressed with you."

"No, it's okay," Dix said. "How's the wine?"

"Good."

"Save a little room for the pie," Dix said. "I asked for real whipped cream."

"I've only had that once," Trixie said. "If I remember correctly, it's pretty good."

After dinner, Dix cleared the table by putting the plates onto the serving trolly, then he and Trixie had pie with whipped cream.

Afterward, Trixie said, "Now what? Do you wish me to go since I can't . . . you know?"

"No," Dix said. "Stay and get a good

night's sleep. There are two beds, pick one."

"By the window," Trixie said. "I like fresh air at night."

Dix sat in a chair and rolled a cigarette and lit it with a wood match. "Tomorrow, I'll pick up a new batch of warrants and head out again."

"Where do you live?" Trixie said. "I mean when you're not working."

"Nowhere," Dix said.

"You must have a home? Somewhere," Trixie said.

"Six years ago I did," Dix said. "After the war, I worked for the railroad as a railroad police officer. Then as a deputy sheriff in Denver. Married a young woman named Victoria. I was away taking a prisoner to Cheyenne when outlaws robbed the bank in Denver. A stray bullet killed my wife."

Trixie stared at Dix from where she was sitting on the bed.

"After that, I became a warrant office and I've been doing that ever since," Dix said.

"For the last six years, you haven't had a place to live?" Trixie said.

"Another two years and I'll have enough put away to buy a ranch somewhere," Dix said. "Montana or Wyoming, maybe."

Trixie turned down her bed and removed her dress. Dix looked at the bruises on her legs and arms.

"It's not pretty, huh," Trixie said.

"But you are," Dix said.

"I thank you for that," Trixie said as she got into her bed.

Dix stood up and removed his shirt and pants. He turned the lantern to low and turned down the covers on his bed.

"I guess we could use some sleep," he said and got into bed.

"Dix, how many men have you killed?" Trixie said.

"I never did figure," Dix said.

"About."

"Maybe sixty in the war," Dix said. "Twenty or so with the railroad and at least two dozen as a warrant officer."

"More than sixty men," Trixie said.

"I guess."

"How come you aren't hard and mean?" Trixie said. "I would think all that killing would make a man as hard as tree bark."

"I try to not let it get to me," Dix said. "I keep sight of the ranch I want to have and it keeps me focused. What about you?"

"You mean, how did I wind up a whore in a Washington saloon?" Trixie said. Before the war, when I was nine or ten, I lived with my parents and two brothers on a farm in Ohio. We were poor. Scratch poor. One day, this wagon stops on the farm. My pa makes a deal with this man and his women and sells me for two-hundred-dollars. I went to work doing and fetching for the man and his whores. We went west when the war broke out and by the time I was fourteen, he had me servicing men for fifty cents apiece. After the war, we came to Washington and he was killed in a knife fight. I'm doing the only thing I know how to do to get by."

Dix sighed into the darkness.

"Don't feel sorry for me, Dix. I don't feel sorry for myself," Trixie said. "It's just the way things are is all."

"I guess you could say the same for me," Dix said.

"Good night, Dix," Trixie said.

"Good night."

Dix fell asleep and woke up sometime during the night when Trixie got into bed with him.

He awoke in the morning with her arms wrapped around him.

Chapter Ten

Dix was on the train west with ten new warrants in his pocket. He organized them according to the bounty offered by the court. The first stop was Dodge Coty, Kansas.

The outlaw Pike Bigelow was reported to be hiding in Dodge or close to it somewhere. Bigelow robbed a bank in Oklahoma and avoided a posse and made it into Kansas. He got away with twelve-thousand-dollars and killed three men in the process.

The bounty on his head was twenty-five-hundred, dead or alive.

The ride to Dodge City was scheduled for thirty plus hours and he reserved a sleeper car for the trip. He didn't have breakfast, so by noon he was famished and had lunch in the dining car.

After that, there wasn't much to do so he went to his sleeper car and read a newspaper.

After that, he fell asleep, sort of. It was a

light sleep where he was conscious enough to feel the rocking of the train, yet still dream.

He felt Trixie's warmth beside him and could smell the soap she used on her hair. The slowing of the train woke him up. They reached a water stop. He got out of bed, sat in a chair and rolled a cigarette.

For such a hard life, Trixie wasn't bitter. She even took the beating she suffered from Post in stride and didn't seek the revenge he got for her.

The train started moving again. He went to the dining car for a pot of coffee, returned to his sleeper car and read the warrants and planned his moves for the next few months while he drank coffee and smoked another cigarette.

Trixie didn't look anything like his wife, but she reminded him of her in that they both had the same easy way about them, were quick to smile and never complained about things that went wrong or sought to pass blame when they did.

Dix read the warrant for Bigelow again. The man to see in Dodge City was Wyatt Earp.

At a table in the rear of the saloon, Trixie took coffee with Angel. The saloon didn't open until noon and then only for lunch until two. After that, liquor was served, but the girls didn't go to work until six, a requirement by the politicians, even though they were the best customers.

Angel smoked a thin cigar as they drank coffee.

"That man Dix has a thing for you," Angel said. "I saw it in his eyes when I told him that no good bastard Post beat you. I saw it again when he beat the living hell out of Post."

"I think he would defend any woman, even us," Trixie said.

"So you have nothing special with him?" Angel said.

"He's gone, Angel," Trixie said. "Who knows when he'll be back."

"But he'll be back and when he does, would you mind if I had a turn with him?" Angel said.

"If that's what he wants, no," Trixie said.

Angel sipped coffee and then said, "Good."

The bartender, a fat man everybody called 'Skinny' left the bar and came to the table and looked at Trixie.

"Your face is looking some better," Skinny said. "Can you work?"

Trixie nodded. "I can work," she said.

"Six o'clock be ready," Skinny said. "And smell nice and maybe they'll overlook those bruises."

Skinny returned to the bar.

Trixie sipped her coffee.

"I'm going to take a bath," Angel said and left the table.

Trixie watched Angel walk up the stairs and it was an odd thing, but she felt a bit of anger and jealousy at the thought of Dix with Angel.

Chapter Eleven

The train arrived in Dodge City at eight o'clock at night. He walked his horse from the railroad depot to Front Street in the center of town. The street was well-lit with post-mounted lanterns every twenty feet.

The streets were filled with cowboys celebrating a drive, gamblers, drifters and women.

Centered on Front Street was the Dodge Hotel. Dix tied his horse to the hitching rail and entered and went to the desk.

"I need a room," he said. "Not facing the street."

"Two-fifty a night, in advance," the clerk said.

"I'm not sure how long I'll be in town," Dix said. "I'll pay for a week."

Dix gave the clerk a twenty-dollar bill. "Room 217 at the top of the stairs," the clerk said.

"Could you have my bag brought to the

room and I'll be back later," Dix said.

Dix left the hotel and walked along Front Street and paused in front of the Dodge City Police and Marshal's office. Someone was behind a desk. He opened the door and entered.

"I'm looking for the town marshal, would you be him?" Dix said.

"I'm a deputy. If you mean Wyatt Earp, he isn't here at the moment."

"Do you know where I can find him?" Dix said.

"First of all, who are you mister?" the deputy said.

Dix took his badge out of a pocket and pinned it to his shirt. "Federal Warrant Office," he said. "Name is Dix."

The deputy looked at the badge. "Wyatt is at The Long branch Saloon," he said.

"Thank you," Dix said.

The Long Branch Saloon was a block away from the hotel. It was a large saloon with several gambling tables. Earp was dealing Faro at the largest table. Dix walked up to the table and looked at Earp.

"Marshal, a word, please?" Dix said.

Earp looked at Dix's badge. "Grab a drink and a table, I'll be right over," he said.

Dix went to the bar, got a shot of whiskey and found a small, empty table. He rolled a cigarette and waited. Presently, drink in hand, cigar in mouth, Earp came to the table and took a chair.

"Now, Mr. . . . ?" Earp said.

"Dix."

"Mr. Dix, what can I do for you?" Earp said.

Dix removed the folded warrant from his jacket pocket and handed it to Earp. "Pike Bigelow, wanted for triple murder," he said.

"A report claims he was seen in Dodge," Dix said. "Eyewitnesses said he looks like this." Dix removed a folded paper from the same pocket and handed it to Earp.

"I know this man," Earp said. "For the past three months, he comes to town on Saturday night for a little drinking and gambling. He's sat at my faro table on more than one occasion. Calls himself Pete Briggs. I never asked where he lives."

"Tomorrow is Saturday," Dix said.

"So it is," Earp said.

"I'll take him on the street if you're inclined to point him out to me," Dix said. "I'd like to avoid any shooting in a crowded saloon."

"Right considerate of you," Earp said. "If you'd like to sit in, the cards are hot and we have some fine sporting ladies upstairs."

"I believe I'll return to my hotel, get a bite

and some sleep," Dix said. "It was a long train ride."

Dix sipped a small shot of whiskey and smoked a cigarette as he looked out the window that overlooked the back alley of the hotel. Away from Front Street, the music from the saloons was soft and hushed. The alley was dark and quiet.

For a moment, he wondered how Trixie was doing.

"No," he said aloud. "Do not fall for a whore. She'll only break your heart."

Chapter Twelve

Dix and Earp sat in chairs on the wood sidewalk in front of the Long Branch Saloon. Each had a cup of coffee and smoked a cigar. Dix toyed with a rope.

Earp's five deputies were positioned on the sidewalk and street so they blended in with the street traffic.

The sun was going down and the streets were darkening. Two men with torches and stepladders were lighting the street lanterns.

Without raising his voice, Earp said, "That's him on the big paint."

Dix looked at the massive man on the big paint. Pike Bigelow had to weigh two-fifty or more. He carried .44 Schofield revolver on his right hip.

"There's a lot of people on the street," Earp said. "He starts shooting, someone could get hit. Let my deputies surround him when he dismounts."

Bigelow rode to the hitching post and

dismounted. He tied the reins to the post, turned and stepped toward the Long branch Saloon.

Dix was out of his chair and with reflexes like a cat, tossed the lasso over Bigelow's chest and yanked tight, pinning his arms to his side.

"Hey what?" Bigelow said as Dix drew his Colt and smacked Bigelow across the head with it, knocking him unconscious to the ground.

Earp hadn't moved a muscle. Dix looked at Earp's five deputies as they surrounded Bigelow.

Earp stood up and walked beside Dix. "Take him to jail, boys," he said to his deputies. "The charge is murder times three."

"I want that rope back," Dix said to the deputies.

"Well Mr. Warrant Officer, buy you a drink?" Earp said.

In the morning, Dix and Earp had breakfast at the café in the hotel lobby.

"Your train to Oklahoma leaves at ten," Earp said. "You'll be there by four o'clock."

"Appreciate all your hospitality and your help," Dix said.

"Hospitality is free and it was a pleasure watching you work," Earp said. "Bigelow is waiting for you at the depot."

They walked to the depot where Dix's horse and Bigelow waited. Bigelow's wrists and angled were in shackles. A sixteen-pound ball was attached to the chain around his waist and he was holding it.

"You'll never get me there," Bigelow said.

"Wanna bet," Dix said.

Earp and Dix shook hands. "Have a good trip, Dix," Earp said.

Dix walked Bigelow through the streets of Tulsa where the county courthouse was located. The population was just five hundred people, but it seemed as if every one of them was in the street watching Dix walk Bigelow to the courthouse.

Dix turned Bigelow over to a marshal, then went to see the judge in his chambers.

"I don't know how you did it, son, but that son of a bitch will hang," the judge said.

Dix was on the six o'clock train to Joplin, Missouri to serve the second of the ten warrants.

Chapter Thirteen

Seven weeks after the incident in Dodge City, Dix took three different railroads to reach Rapid City in South Dakota.

From Rapid City, Dix had to ride his horse forty miles through the Black Hills on the stagecoach road. His horse had quite a bit of rest the past several weeks and needed a good stretch of the legs, so Dix left Rapid City at seven in the morning and covered the forty miles in just four hours.

Along the way he passed a stagecoach full of passengers and several freight wagons. One freight wagon was driven by a man, but a woman dressed in men's clothing rode shotgun.

As he rode past the freight wagon, the woman yelled, "Hey you shitbird, who you think you passing?" Then she stood up, dropped her pants, turned and smacked herself on the butt. "Kiss this, shitbird," she yelled.

Dix ignored the obviously drunk woman and rode on.

He arrived in Deadwood an hour later. Constructed in the Black Hills, Deadwood was long and narrow as towns go. The streets were muddy, the shops crowded, the pace chaotic and it was the ideal place for an outlaw to hide out in because nobody would care.

As he rode through the main thoroughfare, Dix passed two fat mem fighting in the mud, several women nearly naked sitting on milk boxes, drinking whiskey, a half-crazed man preaching the Bible, a Chinese man chasing a pig with a meat clever. A man on his knees, vomiting into the mud, the Nuttal Saloon where Bill Hickock was murdered, The Gem Saloon where a man was drinking coffee on the balcony and finally the sheriff's office.

Dix dismounted in front of the sheriff's office, tied his horse to a post, stepped onto the wood sidewalk and tried the door. It was locked.

"Sheriff ain't in," a woman sitting on a milk crate said. "But for a dollar, I'll tell you where he is."

Dix found a dollar coin in a pocket and flipped it to the woman. "Go back the way you came to the Starr and Bullock Hardware Store. You'll find him there," the woman said.

"Thanks," Dix said.

He mounted the saddle and rode back and stopped in front of the hardware store and dismounted. On the sidewalk, an angry man was waving a Bowie knife at a tall, thin man dressed in a suit.

"You cheating Jew, I want my money back or I'm gonna gut you like a fish," the man with the Bowie knife said.

"Seth," the man in the suit said.

The man with the Bowie knife lunged at the man wearing the suit. Dix drew his Colt and whacked the man with the knife on the wrist. He dropped the knife and Dix cracked the man across the jaw with his Colt. The man fell to the wood sidewalk.

A man in a suit, with a walrus moustache came from somewhere in the store. "What is it, Sol?" he said.

"Never mind," Sol said.

"I'm looking for the sheriff," Dix said.

"You found him. I'm Seth Bulloch, sheriff of Deadwood," Bulloch said. "And you are?"

Dix had his badge pinned to his shirt, but his vest covered it. He moved the vest out of the way so Bulloch could see it. "Federal Warrant Officer Dix. Can we talk for a minute?" Dix said.

"Sol, watch the store," Bullock said. He stepped over the unconscious man. "And get this asshole out of here and tell him to never come back."

Bulloch led Dix across the street to a large, crowded café. As they entered, Bullock said, "Johnny, two cups of coffee if you please."

They grabbed a vacant table and Johnny brought over two cups of coffee. "So, what does a Federal Warrant Officer want in Deadwood?" Bulloch said.

Dix removed a warrant from his pocket and handed it to Bulloch. "John Grimes, wanted for murder, robbery, rape, extortion, assault and gun running," Bulloch said. "And let me guess, you think he's hiding here in Deadwood."

"The dumb son of a bitch wrote a letter to his brother telling him he staked a claim in the hills and asked him to join him," Dix said.

"And his brother turned him in for the reward?" Bulloch said.

"His brother found religion and married a Mormon girl," Dix said. "He turned him in, but not for the reward."

Bulloch sipped his coffee. "Religion is a wonderful thing," he said.

Dix removed the poster with Grimes' face on it and handed it to Bulloch. "He's been in my store. Several times. I believe he bought on credit, which means whatever name he is using is in my books."

"And that name would be on his claim," Dix said.

"Correct," Bulloch said. "My partner Sol keeps the books."

Sol Starr looked at the poster and said, "Yeah, he bought on credit. Paid it back, too. Bought several pick axes, lanterns, shovels and . . ."

"Sol, we don't care what he bought," Bulloch said. "We care what name he used."

"Oh," Sol said. "James Gallo."

"Thanks, Sol," Bulloch said.

Bulloch and Dix returned to the street. "Claims office is right up the street," Bulloch said.

They walked along the wood sidewalk and passed the two fat men that were fighting and now lay unconscious in the mud.

"Who runs this town?" Dix said.

"The mayor is E.B. Farnum," Bulloch said. "He owns the hotel. The man with the most power is Al Swearengen and he owns the Gem Saloon. That's him up on the balcony across the street."

Dix glanced up at the balcony. It was the man drinking coffee.

They stopped at the claims office and entered. A man was behind a counter. Several men stood in line.

"Earl, I need a claim number and location," Bulloch said.

"Name?" Earl said.

"Gallo," Bulloch said.

"The book under G," Earl said.

Bulloch went to a bookshelf behind the counter. Dix followed. Bulloch removed the book titled G and opened it.

"Gallo, James," Bulloch said. "His claim is about fourteen miles to the east."

"Thanks. I best go get him," Dix said.

"Wait until tomorrow and I'll go with you," Bulloch said.

"I can go alone."

"You don't understand," Bulloch said. "There might be thirty, fifty men working claims with him. They don't like law. Any one of those crazy bastards might open up on you. You'll need backup. Check into the hotel, have dinner with me tonight and we'll formulate a plan for tomorrow."

"Alright, sheriff," Dix said.

"Let's get your horse stabled and we'll go to the hotel," Bulloch said.

■ ■ ■ ■

"E.B., this is Federal Warrant Officer Dix," Bulloch said. "Give him the best room you got."

Farnum looked across the desk at Dix. "Would you want a shave and a bath?" he said.

"I would and I have some laundry needs washing," Dix said.

"Seven o'clock right here for supper," Bulloch said.

When Dix arrived at a table at the hotel dining room, Bulloch, Sol Starr, Charlie Utter and Al Swearengen were already seated.

"You know my partner Sol," Bulloch said. "This is Charlie Utter and Al Swearengen. Charlie, Al, Mr. Dix."

"We understand we have a murderer in camp," Swearengen said. "That won't do. It's bad for the camp's reputation."

"I've deputized Sol and Charlie as my deputies," Bulloch said. "And as much as it pains me to say this, Jane Canary."

"A woman?" Dix said.

"Calamity Jane," Bulloch said. "And here she comes now."

Jane came to the table and looked at Dix.

"You're that shitbird what passed me on the road this morning," she said.

"That's no way to talk to a Federal Warrant Officer, Jane," Swearengen said.

"What's that?" Jane said as she took a chair.

"What that is, Jane, is the power to shut this entire camp down if he so chooses," Swearengen said. "So behave yourself."

Jane looked at Dix. "He reminds me of Wild Bill," she said.

"He doesn't look anything like Bill," Bulloch said.

"I said reminds, not looks, you moustache wearing shitbird," Jane said.

"Mr. Dix, I employ professional bodyguards and I am donating the services of two of them to escort you tomorrow," Swearengen said. "With your permission, of course."

A waiter came to the table. They ordered dinner and a bottle of whiskey. The bottle came first and everybody had a drink.

Dix sipped his drink and looked at Swearengen. "I'm curious, Mr. Swearengen as to why a saloon owner needs bodyguards," he said.

"Quite simple, Mr. Dix," Swearengen said. "In this camp, you could get your throat cut for a nickel and I have a lot of nickels."

Dix turned to Bulloch. "Sheriff, do you know the exact location of Grimes' claim?"

"Who's Grimes?" Jane said. "I thought we were after this Gallo prick."

"That's his real name, Jane," Bulloch said. "To answer your question, Mr. Dix, I know the exact location. It's a bit over fourteen miles into the hills."

"We'll leave an hour before sunup," Dix said. "I find it easier to take a man before he's fully awake."

"What time is sunup?" Jane said.

"Around six-thirty," Bulloch said.

"Most nights I ain't even gone to bed yet," Jane said.

"Then it should be no problem for you, Jane," Bulloch said.

The waiter arrived with dinner.

"Bring us another bottle," Jane said.

Dix was undressing and about to go to bed when there was a knock on the door. He took his Colt to the door and opened it. A blonde woman in seductive clothes looked at him.

"Yes?" Dix said.

"Mr. Swearengen sent me," she said.

"What for?" Dix said.

"Keep you company."

"Tell Mr. Swearengen that my wife is all the company I need," Dix said.

"You're kidding?"

"No, I'm not," Dix said. "Good night."

"Well I'll be damned," the woman said.

Chapter Fourteen

Dix met Bulloch in front of his hardware. Sol Starr and Charlie Utter were with him. They were drinking coffee.

"Sol, a cup for Mr. Dix," Bulloch said.

Sol went into the store and returned with a cup for Dix. "Thank you," Dix said.

Two burly men walked their horses from across the street. "That's Johnny and Dan, two of Swearingen's men," Bulloch said.

From the other end of the street, Jane rode her horse slowly as she drank from a whiskey bottle. She tossed the bottle into the street when she arrived. "Let's go if we're going," she said.

Led by Bulloch, they covered the fourteen miles in less than an hour. Each carried a lit torch until it was light enough to see, then they extinguished them.

From a vantage point on top of a tall hill, they dismounted.

Below in a clearing near a stream were

thirty or more tents. Some men were in front of the tents with fires going and coffee boiling.

Dix used his binoculars to zoom in on the faces of the men. "I don't see him yet," he said.

Jane reached into a pocket for a chaw and bit off a piece.

"What do you got there?" Charlie said.

"Licorice," Jane said.

"Give me a chaw," Charlie said.

Jane handed it to Charlie, who took a bite and returned it to Jane.

"There," Dix said. "He just came out of a tent."

Dix returned the binoculars to his saddle-bags. "Get your rifles ready and wait here," he said.

"You're not going down there alone," Bulloch said.

Dix mounted his horse and rode around a bend and down the hill.

"Man's crazy you ask me," Jane said.

"Get your rifles ready," Bulloch said.

As he neared the bottom of the hill, Dix tugged the reins and the horse broke into a run.

"What the hell's he doing?" Charlie said.

As he reached the tents, Dix aimed his horse at Grimes and Grimes threw himself to the ground.

Everybody in the camp froze in place as Dix circled back and charged Grimes a second time. Just about to stand up, Grimes was knocked down again.

Dix dismounted with his rope in hand. He grabbed the gun from Grimes's holster and tossed the rope around his neck.

"Who are you? What I do?" Grimes said.

"Shut up," Dix said as he mounted his horse.

"Any man thinking of shooting me in the back, take a look at those six rifles on the hill," Dix said. He tugged the reins. "Horse, let's go.

Dragging Grimes, Dix rode back up the hill.

"Come and see and I saw," Charlie said. "A tall man on a pale horse and hell followed with him."

"What are you talking about, Charlie?" Jane said.

"The Bible, Jane," Bulloch said. "The Book of Revelation."

"What's he talking about Revelation?" Jane said.

"Hey, I'm Jewish," Sol said.

Dix reached the top of the hill with Grimes dragging behind him. Dix dismounted and went to the edge and looked down. He cupped his hands and shouted, "You men, saddle his horse and ride it up here. You got five minutes."

Grimes stood up. :Whatever you think I did, I'm innocent," he said.

"Everybody is innocent," Dix said. "Of something. It's what we're guilty of that counts and in that regard, you are as guilty as sin."

A rider brought Grimes' horse up the hill.

"Get on your horse, Grimes," Dis said. "You'll be a guest of Sheriff Bulloch for tonight. Tomorrow we start for Utah."

Bulloch, Sol, Jane, Charlie Utter and Swearengen sat at a table in the Gem Saloon, each with a shot glass of whiskey.

"I never saw a man so bold as what he did this morning," Charlie said. "And I knew Wild Bill a long time and even he wouldn't have done such a crazy stunt."

"Sounds to me like the man doesn't regard his own life," Swearengen said. "I knew a few like that back east."

"You ask me he's just plain crazy," Jane said.

Here he comes now," Bulloch said.

Dix arrived at the table. "He's locked up for the night, sheriff," he said. "Do you have a deputy to stand watch until morning."

"I'll be sleeping in the jail tonight," Bulloch said. "Sol, you can lock up the store early and get some sleep."

"The train doesn't leave for Utah until six out of Rapid City, so we can all get some extra sleep in the morning," Dix said.

"I can ride with you, to Rapid City" Bulloch said.

"He won't be any trouble," Dix said.

"Al, how about you have your cook fix us some dinner?" Bulloch said.

"Well, Mr. Dix, what would you like?" Swearengen said.

Dix turned Grimes over to two U.S. Marshals at the courthouse in Salt Lake City, Utah. "He give you any trouble?" a marshal said.

Grimes was shackled around the ankles and wrists and held a sixteen-pound ball in his arms that was chained around his waist.

"Not a bit," Dix said.

"I'll get you, Dix," Grimes said. "I swear it. I'll get you. Just wait."

"The only thing waiting for you, Grimes, is a rope," Dix said. "And your maker. Best make terms with your rope and peace with your maker."

Chapter Fifteen

Dix met Judge Pickford in the judge's chambers. Pickford reviewed the ten warrants and approved payments.

"Summer of next year you should have your ranch," Pickford said.

"What do you have new for me?" Dix said.

"Come back in the morning and I'll have a check for you and some new warrants," Pickford said.

"Alright, Judge, I'll see you in the morning," Dix said.

At the hotel, Dix shaved and soaked in a hot bath until the water cooled. Then he dressed in a clean suit, tucked the Derringer into a pocket and walked to the saloon.

It was odd how much he was looking forward to seeing Trixie. The last time he looked forward to seeing a woman was Victoria and she's been gone six years already.

The sun was down and street lanterns

were being lit by a work crew with torches. Street traffic was heavy with people walking and carriages.

The saloon was crowded with DC types when Dix entered. He went to the bar and ordered a shot of whiskey. He rolled a cigarette, lit it with a wood match and then looked up at the balcony.

He didn't see Trixie.

"You," a man behind Dix said.

Dix turned around and looked at Congressman Post, who had a .32 caliber, five-shot revolver aimed at him.

"For that beating you gave me," Post said and shot Dix in the chest.

Dix hit the bar, dropped his drink and cigarette and Post fired four more times.

Still on his feet, Dix slowly sank to the floor as men in the bar grabbed Post and shoved him to the floor.

Dix looked up and saw Trixie running down the stairs. Then he closed his eyes.

Doctor Gayland Carver, a surgeon and general practitioner was having a quiet drink with a few colleagues from Capitol Hill Hospital also had an office just one block away from the saloon.

Carver examined Dix quickly and said, "By God, he's still alive. My office is closer, some of you men get him there right now."

Chapter Sixteen

Carver operated on Dix for five hours. His regular nurse assisted. He removed the five bullets and stitched Dix up, but Dix had lost a great deal of blood and was very weak.

Around three in the morning, Carver left his nurse with Dix and went to the waiting room where Trixie and Judge Pickford were asleep in chairs.

"And who are you people?" Carver said.

Pickford opened his eyes. "Judge Pickford. Is he alive?"

"I don't know how, but yes," Carver said. "Five bullets and half the blood in his body gone and he's still alive."

Trixie opened her eyes and looked at Carver. "Is he . . . ?" she said.

"Alive?" Carver said. "Yes, but very weak."

"Oh thank God," Trixie said.

"Who are you, miss?" Carver said.

"I'm his lady friend, Patricia," Trixie said.

"Well, Judge, Patricia, there is nothing

more to do tonight," Carver said. "Come back tomorrow."

"Can I . . . can I sit with him for a while?" Trixie said.

Carver was at his desk with a cup of morning coffee when Judge Pickford entered the office.

"I stopped by to see if he was still alive," Pickford said.

"He is. Don't ask me how or why, but he is," Carver said. "He has the strongest will to live I have ever seen. Now, mind me asking why a federal judge is interested in him? Is he a criminal?"

"He is a Federal Warrant Officer, an officer of the federal court," Pickford said. "He has brought more than one hundred and fifty outlaws to justice and primarily working alone."

"I see," Carver said. "Was it an outlaw that shot him?"

"No. It was a sitting congressman," Pickford said.

"A . . . why?"

"That's what I'd like to find out," Pickford said. "Is he awake?"

"Let's find out," Carver said.

Carver led Pickford to the back room where Dix was in bed. He wasn't awake and neither was Trixie, who spent the night in a chair.

"She been here all night?" Pickford said.

"Never left that chair," Carver said. He gently nudged Trixie awake. "Miss, I have to check Mr. Dix now."

Trixie nodded and stood up.

"Miss, I'm Judge Pickford. We met last night," Pickford said. "I'd like to ask you a few questions. May we have breakfast together?"

Pickford took Trixie to a small café on the hill. He had brought his personal carriage and the morning air seemed to revive her.

Over breakfast, Pickford asked some questions.

"Something tells me you know why Congressman Post shot Mr. Dix," Pickford said.

"I might as well tell you the truth," Trixie said. "I work in a saloon. When Dix comes to town, we see each other. He is a very kind and caring man. I guess it's about three months now, on his last trip to Washington that Dix came to see me."

Trixie paused to sip some coffee.

"Go on," Pickford said.

"Congressman Post is a regular," Trixie said. "He likes to hit woman. He beat me up pretty badly."

"Congressman Post did?" Pickford said.

"And others," Trixie said. "Dix found about it and beat the tar out of Post."

"So Post shot him five times out of revenge?" Pickford said.

"Is he going to get away with it? Politicians tend to get away with everything," Trixie said.

"Not this time," Pickford said. "Not in my court he won't."

"Good. I'm a witness if you need me. I saw the whole thing," Trixie said.

"I will have the prosecutor get in touch with me," Pickford said. "Can I take you someplace?"

"The saloon. I have a room there. I want to pick up a few things," Trixie said.

Trixie entered the saloon with Pickford through the rear entrance. The bartender named Marty said, "Trixie, where you been?"

Trixie ignored him and went up the stairs.

"Hey, you stinking bitch, where do you . . ." Marty said.

"Mister, I'm Federal Judge Pickford," Pickford said. "One more word out of you and I will have this place condemned and you arrested. Am I clear?"

■ ■ ■ ■

When Dix opened his eyes briefly, Trixie was in a chair and holding her hand.

"Hey," he said weakly.

"Trixie smiled. "Hey," she said and Dix fell back asleep.

In Carver's office, he spoke with Pickford. "I give her high marks for dedication, but I can't have her living in the room with him," Carver said.

"Doctor, she isn't going anywhere and you know it," Pickford said. "I will pay all his medical bills and add five-hundred-dollars for her to stay in the room. Roll in a day bed if you have to, but she stays."

"You're the judge," Carver said.

A little while later, Carver's nurse rolled a day bed into the room.

"What's that for?" Trixie said.

"We can't have you sleeping in a chair the whole time," the nurse said. "Give me a hand, would you?"

Chapter Seventeen

Dix was sitting up in bed when Trixie carried a tray into the room and set it across his lap. "Beef broth, bread and coffee," she said.

"Broth?" Dix said.

"Doctor's orders," Trixie said as she took her chair.

"I want a steak," Dix said.

"Finish all that and I'll ask Doctor Carver," Trixie said.

Dix ripped off a hunk of bread, dunked it into the broth and popped it into his mouth. "Oh, God," he said.

"Behave yourself or I won't give you a sponge bath," Trixie said.

"Yes nurse," Dix said.

Carver entered the room with Pickford. "You have a visitor," Carver said and left the room.

"Judge, could you smuggle in a steak with potatoes and gravy and some hot biscuits covered in honey?" Dix said.

Pickford looked at Trixie. "Five days ago he was barely alive and now he wants a steak," he said.

"He's not a very good patient," Trixie said.

"Trixie, may I have a word with Dix in private?" Pickford said.

"Certainly," Trixie said and went to the door.

"More bread," Dix said.

"As you wish, sire," Trixie said.

Pickford sat in Trixie's chair. "I deposited the money from the last ten warrants in the bank for you," he said.

"I appreciate that, judge," Dix said.

"I had your horse brought over to my stables," Pickford said. "He'll let them walk him, but he won't let anybody ride him."

"No, he won't."

"Your belongings from the hotel are outside in your satchel," Pickford said. "Now listen to me. You're the best in the business, but you won't be up and around for a while, that much is clear. What else is clear is that Trixie can't live here in this room with you for the next month, so I am giving you the use of my summer cottage on Lake Anna."

"But Judge . . ." Dix said.

"No buts," Pickford said. "I need you. The

court system needs you. The quicker you recover the quicker you get back to work. I've already discussed it with Doctor Carver and he said you can be moved in three days. His nurse will go with you to make sure you're alright. Everything is on one floor, no stairs. Agreed?"

"Alright, Judge," Dix said. "On one condition. I pick when I'm ready to return to work, not the doctor.

"Agreed. Now about Trixie," Pickford said. "She won't go back to the saloon after this. I don't know how she got mixed up in . . ."

"Her father sold her to a traveling pimp when she was just ten or so for two-hundred-dollars," Dix said.

Pickford was speechless for a moment.

"Don't worry, Judge. She won't go back," Dix said. "Now about that steak."

Trixie slept with the lantern on low flame so that she could see Dix during the night. She got out of bed when she heard him moan and she touched his face. He was burning with fever.

She filled a basin with water and wet a facecloth and placed it over his forehead. Then she went to the room next door where Carver's nurse, Julie, was sleeping while Dix was still in Carver's care.

She knocked on the door. "Julie, wake up," Trixie said.

The door opened and Julie, putting on a robe, stepped out.

"Dix has a fever," Trixie said.

"Go back, I'll be right there," Julie said.

Trixie returned to dix and dipped the facecloth in the basin again and placed it on his forehead.

A few minutes later, Julie entered the room with a basin of crushed ice. "Doctor Carver keeps an ice box of crushed ice for fevers," she said. "Get some towels and facecloths."

They filled a pillow case with ice and placed it over Dix's chest and wrapped ice in a face cloth and put it across his forehead.

"Most times, a patient recovering from a bullet wound will develop a fever during the first week," Julie said. "And he's got five."

"What do we do now?" Trixie said.

"Wait for him to start to shiver," Julie said.

Five minutes or so later, Dix began to shiver. "Remove the towel and let him warm up a bit," Julie said.

They sat in chairs for a few minutes and then Julie felt Dix's forehead. "Another round of ice," she said.

Three rounds of ice later, Julie was satisfied that Dix's fever had broken.

"He'll sleep the night now and I suggest you do the same," Julie said.

"Thank you. Good night," Trixie said.

"Honey, when he gets better, you're going to have a man on your hands," Julie said. "Whether you want him or not."

Chapter Eighteen

Dix and Trixie drove one carriage to Pickford's lakeside cottage, while Doctor Carver and Julie followed in another.

The ride took two days and they stayed overnight at an inn halfway to the lake. While Dix was still weak and somewhat unsteady, he was in fine appetite and got to eat the steak for dinner he was craving for a week.

They reached Pickford's cottage around five o'clock the following afternoon. On the way in, they stopped at a general store for supplies.

The cottage had three bedrooms. Carver and Julie each took a bedroom. Dix took the third and Trixie slept on a roll-away bed next to Dix.

After three days, Carver and Julie pronounced Dix well enough to stay alone with Trixie. "I advise you to take it easy and rest as much as possible and I will return in two weeks," Carver said.

"Doctor, about your bill," Dix said.

"We'll discuss that when I return," Carver said, failing to mention Pickford had paid him in full.

After Carver and Julie left, Dix and Trixie decided on a picnic lunch by the water. Trixie packed roast beef sandwiches, with apples, peaches and a bottle of wine.

They spread a blanket near the water and ate lunch under a clear, blue sky.

"Doctor Carver said you have the constitution of an ox," Trixie said. "And I believe him. Not ten days ago, I saw you shot five times and here we are eating sandwiches beside a lake."

"If he had a .44 instead of a ,32, it would be a different story," Dix said.

"Judge Pickford said that Post could get fifteen years or more," Trixie said.

"He deserves twice that for beating up women," Dix said.

"Julie said when you get well I'll have a man on my hands," Trixie said. "Do I?"

"That depends on if you want one," Dix said.

Trixie looked at the calm waters of the lake. The sun reflected off it and the water glistened. "Men have this rule," she said. "Oh, it's not written down anywhere and they don't speak of it and it's not taught in school, but they have it none the less. It's the never fall for a whore rule. Ever hear of it?"

"Ever hear of rules were meant to be broken?" Dix said.

"Are you saying you want me?" Trixie said.

"If you'll have me," Dix said.

"If I'll have . . . "Trixie said and hugged Dix.

"Ouch," Dix said.

"Sorry."

Dix got on his back and looked up at the sky. "I have to work at least another year," he said. "Maybe longer. To start a ranch, I'll need the land, a house, barn, bunkhouse, corral, horses and cattle. I need fifty-thousand. Sixty would be better. I have forty."

"I have a thousand squirreled away, you can have it," Trixie said.

"Keep that for an emergency," Dix said.

"Are we talking real or are we just talking?" Trixie said.

"The last trip, the entire time I kept telling myself not to fall in love with a saloon girl," Dix said. "The day I got back, I went to the saloon to tell you just that. Post shot me before I got the chance."

Trixie got beside Dix and took his hand. “When I saw you I came running down the stairs,” she said. “I saw him take out the gun and I froze on the stairs and watched him shoot you over and over. It only took a few seconds, but it seemed like an eternity.”

“That happens in war,” Dix said. “When the bullets star to fly, everything slows down to a crawl.”

“A silly question, but while you’re off working the next year or so, what am I doing?” Trixie said.

“I can tell you what you’re not doing and that’s working in a saloon,” Dix said.

“Dix, half of congress knows me,” Trixie said. “I’m going to be recognized.”

“The hell with all of them,” Dix said. “In eighteen months, we’ll be out west living on our ranch.”

“Do you think you can . . . I mean are you strong enough to . . . you know?” Trixie said.

“Let’s go find out,” Dix said.

Chapter Nineteen

Trixie opened her eyes to the sound of wood being chopped and the aroma of fresh coffee. She got out of bed, went to the kitchen for a cup of coffee and then looked out the kitchen window at Dix as he chopped wood.

He was shirtless and his muscles glistened from a film of sweat in the morning sun. Three weeks ago, he was knocking on death's door, today he's swinging an ax.

She opened the window. "Hey crazy man, want breakfast?" she said.

Dix paused, looked at her and said, "Call me when it's ready."

Trixie prepared biscuits, put bacon to fry, made some hashbrown potatoes fried in butter and called Dix in just before she scrambled some eggs. He washed up at the pimp in the yard and then came to the table.

"I need to check those wounds and make sure none of them are going to bleed," Trixie said.

"I'm fine," Dix said.

Trixie glared at him.

"Okay, let me eat first before you go poking around."

"I'm going to boil water for a bath," Trixie said.

The tub in the barn behind the cottage was large enough for two and Dix and Trixie soaked in scented, hot water. Trixie checked the five gunshot wounds. "Skin is still tender, but healing pretty good," she said. "What's these other two here on the left side?"

"Rebel bullets from the war," Dix said.

"And this puncture on the right shoulder?"

"A Ute arrow."

"And this one your right upper back?"

"A Cherokee tomahawk from when I worked for the railroad."

"Your scars are like a roadmap," Trixie said.

"We all have scars," Dix said.

"Mine are on the inside," Trixie said.

"That's in the past," Dix said. "For both of us. We can't start out together carrying scars around like it was a bag of bricks."

"What's it like out Montana and Wyoming way?" Trixie said.

"You could ride for two weeks and not see another person in Montana," Dix said. "The sky is extra blue and so wide it's blinding. Most of Wyoming is the same way. It's perfect cattle country."

Trixie rested her head against the rim of the tub. "I'll go anywhere you say," she said. "Anywhere at all."

Chapter Twenty

Dix took the buggy to town for another week's worth of supplies. He would be gone at least three hours. Trixie used the time to do some laundry in the large basin outside the barn.

She washed their dirty laundry, the linen and towels. Inside the barn was a woodstove where water heated.

She heard a horse, turned and expected to see Dix returning from town. Instead she saw two men dismounting from their horses.

"Hello, little mama," one of the men said. "Is your man around?"

"What do you want?" Trixie said.

"Water our horses," the second man said.

"There's an entire lake not a hundred yards from here," Trixie said.

"Our horses like their water from a well," the first man said.

"There's a pump, help yourself," Trixie said.

"Where's your man?" the first man said.

"In the house, want me to call him?" Trixie said.

The two men walked to Trixie, who didn't back away. One of them looked in the barn. "No horse, no man," he said.

The second man grabbed Trixie.

"Not out in the open, in the barn," the second man said.

"I'll scratch and I'll bite," Trixie said. "You might get your way, but you'll be bleeding when you leave."

"You do that, pretty mama," the first man said. "A little blood never hurt nothing now and again."

"I'd let her go if I was you," Dix said from behind the two men. "Or it will be a lot of blood and all of it yours."

"Hi," Trixie said. "I saw you from a ways off."

"You alright?" Dix said.

"We ain't hurt her none," the first man said.

"We're just watering our horses," the second man said.

"By grabbing my wife?" Dix said. "Trixie, back away a bit."

The two men looked at Dix's Colt on his hip.

"Right behind the barn is going to be two

freshly dug graves," Dix said. "A cheap marker will have the words Rest in Pieces, carved in it."

"Now hold on, mister," the first man said. "We ain't no gunmen."

"Let's find out," Dix said. "I'll give you a count of three to draw."

"We're going, mister," the second man said.

"One," Dix said.

"You hear me, we're going," the second man said.

Two," Dix said.

"You can't do this," the first man said. "We ain't no gunmen."

"Three," Dix said.

The two men reached for their guns, but before they could clear leather, Dix had his Colt out, cocked and aimed.

"On your horses," Dix said. "If either of you double back, I'll kill the both of you on sight."

The two men ran to their horses, mounted up and raced away from the barn.

Dix holstered his Colt and walked to Trixie.

"You alright?" he said.

Trixie nodded. "You called me your wife," she said.

"That's how I think of you," Dix said.

"Did you get all the supplies?"

"I did."

"Bring them in the house," Trixie said. "I'll finish up here and fix you a nice supper."

In front of the fireplace, Trixie and Dix made love under a thick blanket.

"I'd say you were at full strength," Trixie said.

Dix sat up and rolled a cigarette. "I need to get back to work, so we can get our ranch," he said.

Trixie stood up, tossed on her robe and went to the kitchen. I'll get dinner started," she said.

Dix was sound asleep beside her, but Trixie was wide awake even though it was after midnight.

She knew sleep wouldn't come.

Not tonight.

She knew the day would come when Dix was ready to return to work, but she didn't count on how quickly he would recover.

Trixie got out of bed, lit a lantern and went to the kitchen and sat at the table.

She was being selfish, she knew, but she didn't want him leaving her to go off and possibly get killed by some outlaw.

Dix entered the kitchen. "What is it?" he said.

"Can't sleep," Trixie said.

Dix took a chair at the table. "What is it?"

"Worry."

"About what?"

"You, what else," Trixie said. "About you leaving and getting killed by some stupid outlaw somewhere and I'll never see you again. That's what."

Dix went to the icebox for the bottle of milk and he poured two glasses and brought them to the table.

"Milk is supposed to help you sleep," he said.

"Maybe I'm being foolish or selfish, but I don't want you getting killed before we even had the chance to live," Trixie said.

"I can't quit now," Dix said. "I need at least ten, maybe twenty-thousand more for us to get a proper start."

"And what kind of start do we have if you're dead?" Trixie said.

"You've got to trust me on this," Dix said.

Trixie sipped some milk. "You'll stop at fifty-thousand?" she said.

"If that's enough," Dix said. "And maybe you can help with that?"

"How?"

"While I'm away you can start pricing land."

"I don't know anything about land," Trixie said.

"You never had the chance to attend school, yet you read and write as well as anybody. How come?" Dix said.

"I taught myself," Trixie said.

"That makes you smarter than most," Dix said. "You can find us the land. Finish your milk, we need some sleep."

"You want me to sleep?" Trixie said. She took Dix by the hand and walked him to the bedroom. "Prove it," she said.

CHAPTER TWENTY-ONE

Trixie was on the porch, shucking a basket of corn when Judge Pickford arrived in a buggy.

He parked the buggy and was greeted warmly with a hug by Trixie.

"The man of the house, how is his recovery coming?" Pickford said.

"Go take a look," Trixie said. :He's around by the barn."

Pickford went around the side of the house where a shirtless Dix was chopping wood. He watched for a moment as Dix loaded a log onto the block and split it with a powerful blow from the ax.

"I see you're looking well," Pickford said.

"Hello, Judge," Dix said.

From the kitchen window, Trixie said, "Come in the house for coffee."

"You heard the boss," Dix said as he grabbed his shirt.

At the kitchen table, Trixie poured three

cups of coffee.

"You're looking well," Pickford said.

"I have a good nurse," Dix said.

"When do you think you'll be ready to return to work?" Pickford said.

"A week."

"There is a lot to do," Pickford said.

"Judge, I'm concerned about Trixie," Dix said. "She can't go back to that saloon and we don't have a place for her to stay while I'm away."

"I've already thought of that, if she's willing," Pickford said.

"Willing to do what?" Trixie said.

"My housekeeper retired," Pickford said. "I provide a comfortable room, require two meals a day and pay twenty-dollars-a week."

"On one condition," Trixie said.

"What's that?"

"You marry us before Dix returns to work," Trixie said.

Pickford looked at Dix.

"You heard the boss," Dix said.

"Marriage has changed a bit in DC," Pickford said. "You now require a license. When you return, fill out the license and I'll marry you two."

"A license?" Dix said.

"A formality," Pickford said. "But I won't marry you without rings, so you'll need to buy a set beforehand."

"Are you staying overnight?" Dix said.

"The trip wore me out," Pickford said. "I believe so."

"Good. Trixie is a hell of a cook," Dix said. "Right now I'll be outside chopping wood."

After Dix leaves the kitchen, Trixie refills Pickford's coffee cup, then her own and sat beside Pickford.

"Judge, what do you know about buying land?" Trixie said.

"Nothing personally," Pickford said. "But I know someone who does. Are you talking about the ranch Dix wants to start?"

"Yes. He's asked me to start pricing land while he's away," Trixie said.

"When I get home, I'll call on my friend," Pickford said.

"Thank you," Trixie said.

"I believe I'll go help Dix for a while," Pickford said. "Some exercise might be just what I need."

As Dix split logs, Pickford picked them up and carried them into the barn. This went on for three hours.

When the last log was split, they went to the pump and filled a bucket with water.

Each poured a ladle of water over their heads.

"I haven't done so much physical work since I can't remember," Pickford said.

"Ready for supper?" Dix said.

"I believe I am," Pickford said.

Trixie prepared fried chicken with corn on the cob and baked an apple pie for dessert. On his trip to the general store, Trixie requested fresh lemons and she made lemonade.

"I know you men are anxious to talk business, so you might as well have at it," Trixie said.

"I admit I'm anxious to have Dix back at work," Pickford said. "The amount of warrants is piling up and there just isn't enough qualified warrant officers to do the job."

"We'll pack up in five days and be there come Sunday," Dix said.

"You can get the license at City Hall on Monday," Pickford said. "Pick up a set of rings and I'll perform the ceremony in my chambers."

"Can I make a request?" Trixie said.

"I don't see why not," Pickford said.

"Dix is bound and determined to see this through until he has enough money to buy a ranch," Trixie said. "But I was wondering if you could arrange it so he isn't away more than a month at a time instead of three or four?"

Pickford looked at Dix. "It might take longer, but I can arrange it," he said.

"I'll put on the coffee and get the pie," Trixie said.

"I'll be back," Dix said. "I have to feed and water the horse."

After Dix left the kitchen, Trixie put the coffee on the woodstove and sliced up the apple pie.

"It's only natural for a woman to worry about the man she loves when the man has a dangerous job," Pickford said. "But, if the man with the dangerous job has to worry about the woman he left behind, he's more likely to become careless and unfocused. Understand?"

Trixie nodded. "Don't let him see me worry," she said.

"Every time he sees you worry, it weakens him a little bit," Pickford said. "And for a man in his position, that is not good."

"He won't see me worry," Trixie said.

"Good," Pickford said.

Dix returned. "I smell coffee and apple pie," he said.

Pickford was alone on the porch, smoking a

cigar. The sun had set and the sky was fading to dark when Trixie came out with two cups of coffee. She gave one to Pickford and then took the chair beside him.

"Where is Dix?" Pickford said.

"I told him to take a bath," Trixie said. "All that sweat from chopping wood today, he smelled like his horse."

"I could use a hot bath myself," Pickford said. "My back isn't as young as it once was."

"I'll put up some water to boil," Trixie said.

"In the morning," Pickford said. "Have you ever heard of the Stock Growers Association?"

"Yes," Trixie said. "They hold conventions in Washington every year and the first thing they do is send for women and most of them are married."

"Granted, some of them let off steam," Pickford said. "However, the president of the association is a friend of mine and he knows more about the land out west than anybody. If anybody can help you and Dix find the right land, it's him. You owe it to Dix to talk to him."

"When can we see him?" Trixie said.

"As soon as I get home, I'll see him," Pickford said.

Fully dressed, Dix returned from the barn. "Nice evening," he said.

"I should spend more time here, but after my wife passed, it didn't seem worth the trouble coming here alone," Pickford said.

"All the more reason you should," Dix said.

"I was wondering, Trixie, if there was another slice of that apple pie?" Pickford said.

Chapter Twenty-Two

"What is it and where did you get it?" Trixie said.

"It's a women's bathing suit and it's for swimming," Dix said. "I got one for me too at the general store."

Trixie picked up the bathing suit from the bed. It was made of heavy wool and had black leggings. "Where's yours?"

Dix removed his from a paper bag and held it up. "We've been at this lake for weeks and not once went into the water," he said. "Let's go for a swim."

"I feel ridiculous in this thing," Trixie said. "I'd rather nothing at all than this silly bath suit."

"Alright," Dix said and started to remove his trunks.

"Don't you dare," Trixie said. "We're in public."

"Well come on then," Dix said.

Dix waded into the lake up to his waist and then dove under. He came up some ten feet from shore, turned and waved to Trixie. "Water's warm. Come on in," he said.

Trixie stuck her right foot in, then her left until she was ankle deep.

"Come on, hon," Dix said.

"Dix . . . I . . . can't," Trixie said.

"Why not?"

"I never learned to swim."

"What?"

"I never learned to swim."

"The water is only up to my waist," Dix said. "Just dive under."

Trixie sighed, then held her breath and dove under the water. She came up flailing her arms. "Dix, where are you?" she said.

"Right here," Dix said and took hold of her waist.

"Don't let me go."

"I won't. Ever."

"Promise?"

"Promise."

"Teach me to swim."

"I'm going to hold out my hands," Dix said. "Float on them."

They sat in the sun by the water's edge to dry off. Dix rolled a cigarette.

"That was fun," Trixie said.

"When you look for our land, make sure it has a river or creek running through it so we can swim on hot summer days," Dix said.

"Dix, there is something else I never learned how to do," Trixie said.

"What's that?"

"Ride a horse proper," Trixie said.

"That's an easy one," Dix said. "Easier than swimming and you learned in one morning. Come on, I want to get some practice in before we lose the sun."

Dix lined up six empty milk bottles on the sawhorse outside the barn. He strapped on his holster and checked the Colt to make sure it was fully loaded.

Trixie stood behind him to the right.

Dix drew the Colt and rapid fired six times, hitting all six bottles. As he reloaded, he said, "Grab three bottles,"

Trixie removed three milk bottles from a wood crate beside the barn.

Reloaded, Dix holstered the Colt. "Throw them as high as you can," he said.

Trixie tossed the three milk bottles into the air. Dix drew and fired three times, shattering all three.

"How many bottles left?" Dix said.

"About a dozen."

"Throw three more," Dix said.

CHAPTER TWENTY-THREE

Dix and Trixie stopped at the inn thirty miles north from Lake Anna. The clerk at the check-in desk remembered them and gave them a large room on the second floor. They had dinner in the dining hall and took coffee on the porch.

"What is it, hon?" dix said. "You barely said two words all day."

"When we get to Washington, you're going off and the thought stuck in my head is you're not coming back," Trixie said.

"We're going to have the judge marry us, why would you think that?" Dix said.

"Because you could be killed," Trixie said.

"Hey, as you witnessed firsthand, I'm not so easy to kill," Dix said. "And I stop as soon as we have enough money to buy our land. Your job is going to be to find it. Agreed?"

Trixie nodded. Agreed," she said.

■ ■ ■ ■

They reached Judge Pickford's large brownstone shortly before sunset. He met them at the door with a hug for Trixie and a handshake for Dix.

"I'll see to the horse and be right in," Dix said.

Pickford's brownstone stood on two acres of wooded property. Besides the house, there was a livery for Pickford's horses, a small barn and toolshed. His nearest neighbor at the end of the block was a doctor.

Dix's horse was excited to see him and kicked at the stall door when Dix put the judge's horse away.

Dix rubbed his neck and then brushed him with a groom's brush.

"We'll be on the road soon enough," Dix said. "I hope you didn't get too fat and lazy while I was away."

The horse snorted as Dix rubbed his neck. "I'll be back later," Dix said.

Pickford had a beautiful home and his wife's presence was felt in every room. He showed Trixie and Dix the house and then the large, housekeeper's room on the second floor.

"My wife decorated this room," Pickford

said. "She died shortly after."

"There are some photographs of your children," Trixie said. "Where are they?"

"My son Charles is a lawyer in Baltimore," Pickford said. "My daughter Rebecca is a school teacher in Pennsylvania."

"Well, to celebrate our first night together, I suggest we dine out tonight," Pickford said.

The restaurant was a short buggy ride from the house and was a small, quiet place where the staff knew the judge well.

"Tomorrow, we'll get the license," Dix said. "When can you marry us?"

"As soon as you get the rings," Pickford said.

"I guess we'll do that tomorrow, too," Dix said.

"I have a full schedule tomorrow, so breakfast at eight." Pickford said.

Trixie nodded. "What would you like?" she said.

"My wife would always ask me that and I would always answer, surprise me," Pickford said.

Chapter Twenty-Four

Trixie prepared what Pickford enjoyed most for breakfast, buttermilk pancakes with bacon and sausage.

He left for court at seven-thirty.

Trixie tidied up the kitchen, then she and Dix took one of Pickford's buggies to the shopping district in downtown Washington.

There was a block with six jewelry stores that Washington regulars called the Diamond District.

They entered three different stores before finding a set of gold bands they were comfortable with. Trixie was a size seven, but Dix was a size fourteen and his ring needed to be fitted.

"It will take about an hour to resize the gentleman's ring," the clerk said.

"That gives us time to shop for the engagement ring," Dix said.

"No, Dix, that's too much . . ." Trixie said.

"Show the lady what you have while I go

to the bank," Dix said.

"If the lady would step this way," the clerk said.

Trixie grinned at hearing the word lady. "Lead the way," she said.

Trixie looked at the diamond ring on her finger as Dix drove the buggy to City Hall. "One hundred and five dollars for one ring," she said. "Honestly, Dix."

"It's not that much when you consider you'll be wearing it the next thirty years," Dix said.

"But . . ." Trixie said.

"We're here," Dix said.

Dix parked the buggy on a sandlot, parking space outside City Hall where thirty or more other buggies were parked. They entered and found the room for marriage licenses on the first floor.

They filled out the required paperwork and left with the license. The federal courthouse was just a few blocks away.

They returned to the buggy and Dix drove them to the courthouse.

"Are you nervous?" Trixie said. "Not at all. You?"

"Scared."

"About us getting married? Why?"

"I'm afraid you'll wake up one day and

realize you married a saloon girl and disappear on me," Trixie said.

"I'm marrying a beautiful woman with the kindest heart I've ever encountered," Dix said. "That's all there is to that. Let's go."

Pickford was in his chambers when Dix and Trixie arrived.

"We have the rings and license," Trixie said.

"Dix, could you get my court officer in here to witness?" Pickford said.

Fifteen minutes later, Dix and Trixie were married.

"A moment with Dix, Trixie," Pickford said.

"I'll wait outside," Trixie said.

"I have two warrants for you," Pickford said. "They're as bad as they come this bunch. Each has a posted reward of twenty-five-hundred. I'll give you the files to take with you. When do you want to leave?'

"Day after tomorrow," Dix said.

"Now don't worry about Trixie," Pickford said. "I'll keep her too busy to worry."

"I appreciate that, Judge."

"Oh, one final thing," Pickford said. "Could you give this list to Trixie for me and stop by the food market on K Street on your way back. I have an account. Just give the list to the manager."

"Sure," Dix said.

"Everything alright?" Trixie said.

"Yeah," Dix said. "We're going grocery shopping."

Chapter Twenty-Five

Dix sat on the back porch of Pickford's home with a cup of coffee, a rolled cigarette and the two files the judge gave him.

The first file was on a man named Stephen Richards out of Nebraska. The sketch showed a handsome, dark-haired man of about thirty. Neighbors described him as charming and friendly. The nine people he was suspected of killing in cold blood would have had a different perspective.

Richard's preferred method of killing was with an ax. He escaped justice and Nebraska and was suspected of hiding in the Arkansas, Ozarks, just northwest of Fort Smith.

The second file was on the Bender Family, an entire family wanted for murder. The ran a small inn near Osage Township in Kansas. The family of four was wanted for the murders of twenty-one guests at their inn.

There was an actual photograph of the

family in front of their inn. They were an evil looking bunch. Before the law could arrest them, they escaped to Missouri, where it was suspected they were living under an assumed name along the Mississippi River south of Saint Louis.

Trixie came out to the porch with a cup of coffee and Dix closed the files. "Is that for the judge?" Trixie said.

"Yeah," Dix said.

"When will you go?"

"Day after tomorrow."

"For how long?"

"A month, like you asked," Dix said. "These two are worth five thousand."

"Five thousand. They must be some bad men."

"They are."

"The judge will be home in four hours," Trixie said. "I thought maybe you might want to make love to your new wife before he gets home?"

Dix stood up. "You thought right," he said.

"That was a fine supper, Trixie," Pickford said. "I'm afraid I might put on some inches around the middle with your cooking."

"Does that mean you don't want the fresh

blueberry pie I made for dessert?" Trixie said.

"I didn't say that," Pickford said.

Trixie grinned. "I'll put the coffee on," she said.

"We'll be in the den," Pickford said.

Pickford and Dix went to the den and closed the door. "You read the files?" Pickford said.

"I did."

"Who first and when?" Pickford said.

"Day after tomorrow and Richards," Dix said.

"Check in with Judge Parker," Pickford said. "If Richards is holed up in the Nation, it's part of Parker's territory."

"I met him a while back," Dix said.

"Billy Cass, of course," Pickford said. "Dix, no need for me to tell you as a married man you have responsibilities beyond yourself now."

"Is that your way of telling me to be careful?" Dix said.

"I know you know what you're doing and you're probably the best in the country at what you do, just don't make her a widow so soon after becoming a bride," Pickford said.

Trixie knocked on the door. "Judge, Dix, coffee and pie is on the table," she said.

"Well, best not keep my waistline waiting," Pickford said.

Chapter Twenty-Six

Dix kissed Trixie goodbye on the front porch, then rode his horse to the railroad station in downtown Washington.

He caught the ten o'clock train to Fort Smith that was scheduled to arrive at two in the morning.

He reserved a sleeper car so he could grab a few hours' sleep. Trixie had prepared a large breakfast, so he skipped lunch and took a nap in his car instead.

After Dix left, Trixie occupied her time with cleaning. She tidied up the kitchen, then swept all the rugs and floors in the house. She worked through lunch, changed all the linen and dusted just about everything on both floors. The afternoon was spent polishing all of the silverware in the kitchen.

Around five o'clock, she set the table and started supper.

The judge came home around six. "Give

me a moment to wash up and change," he said.

While the judge went to his room, Trixie removed the chicken from the oven and carved it up.

"I haven't seen this place so clean in years," the judge said when he entered the dining room.

Trixie served the chicken, with roasted potatoes and carrots, fresh bread with butter and a glass of wine for the judge.

"I'm bringing a guest to dinner tomorrow," Pickford said. "Tom Newhouser, president of the Stock Growers Association. He's agreed to assist you and Dix with finding the right land for a ranch."

"Dix will be pleased if that were possible," Trixie said.

"Don't look so worried," Pickford said. "Dix has brought to justice more outlaws than any ten men and he's always been alright."

Trixie nodded. "What would you like for dinner for Mr. Newhouser tomorrow?" she said.

Dix ate dinner around seven o'clock in the dining car. After his nap, he was wide awake and read a newspaper in his sleeper car to kill some time until the train arrived at two am in Fort Smith.

The news of the day was interesting. The war in South Africa still raged on and thousands died in battle. An inventor named Thomas Edison claimed his electric lightbulb burled for thirteen and a half hours. In Utica, New York, Frank Woolworth opened what he called The Great Five Cents Store, claiming that every item would cost one nickel. In Dayton, Ohio, James and John Ritty patented the first cash register. A woman named Susan B. Anthony was fighting to pass the 19th Amendment.

Done with the newspaper, Dix rolled and lit a cigarette and read the file on Stephen Richards a second time. It was chilling how a man could use an ax to commit murder.

You shoot man, most times he either survives or dies quickly. But an ax requires you to hack away at your victim, chopping until the victim is dead. The terror felt by the victim must be paralyzing, not to mention the flesh and blood left behind.

Richards must be plum crazy. There were no other words to describe him. Crazy, however, didn't mean stupid. If he escaped the law in Nebraska and made his way into the eastern Ozarks, he wasn't stupid by any means.

There was no mention of him ever using a

gun to kill his victims. Chopping them to bits with an ax probably gives him some kind of pleasure that was addicting like opium or laudanum. That meant he wasn't going to stop until caught or killed.

Dix closed the file and slept until the train pulled into the station at Fort Smith. He walked his horse through the quiet, well-lit streets to the Hotel Fort Smith, where he got a room and boarded his horse for the night.

There was nothing else to do, so he went to bed and fell asleep thinking about Stephen Richards.

Chapter Twenty-Seven

Judge Parker read the warrant for Stephen Richards in his chambers. "This crazy son of a bitch is loose in the Indian Nation?" he said.

"Somewhere on the Arkansas side," Dix said. "I doubt he'd risk Oklahoma."

"You're alone?" Parker said.

"I always work alone if I can help it," Dix said.

"This time you can't," Parker said. "Those mountains are no place for a man to wander around in, especially if you're tracking a crazed killer. You need a guide."

"A guide?"

"U.S. Marshal Bass Reeves knows those mountains as well as any of the Five Tribes," Parker said. "He's also a member of the Cherokee Nation. I'll have him here in an hour."

"Alright," Dix said. "I have to send a

telegram home. I'll be back in an hour."

When Dix reported back to Judge Parker, a large black man wearing a U.S. Marshal's badge was in chambers with him.

"Marshal Bass Reeves, this is Federal Warrant Officer Dix," Parker said. "Mr. Dix, I briefed Marshal Reeves, but you can expand later."

"We'll need supplies," Dix said.

"My horse is downstairs," Reeves said.

They walked their horses to the general store on Front Street.

"Any objections to working with my kind?" Reeves said.

"If you mean a black man, the answer is no," Dix said. "I spent three years fighting for the North, then spent four years on the railroad expansion. Some of the best men I ever met were freed slaves."

"I was born a slave," Reeves said. "The Reeves plantation in Arkansas. They moved to Texas and when the war broke out, I escaped and made it north into the Indian Nation. I lived with the Five Tribes for ten years."

"You speak Cherokee?" Dix said.

"And others."

"Think you'll be able to track Richards?"

"If he's still there, I'll find him," Reeves said.

They reached the general store. "Don't skimp on supplies. I'm on expense account," Dix said. "Where's the gunsmith shop? We'll need a few things."

Dix and Reeves rode west out of Fort Smith and headed to the Ozarks.

"Do you know a warrior named Waya?" Dix said.

"I lived with his people for ten years," Reeves said. "You know him?"

Dix told Reeves the story of Billy Cass.

"It sounds like Waya," Reeves said.

"I assume you know the way to their village?" Dix said.

Reeves grinned. "Blindfolded," he said.

"How long to get there?"

"Late afternoon tomorrow," Reeves said.

"When will they know we're coming?"

"Early afternoon tomorrow," Reeves said.

"And my guess is we'll never see a one of them," Dix said.

"Good guess," Reeves said.

Dix stirred a pot of fresh beef stew. "Almost ready," he said. He rolled a cigarette and lit it with a twig from the fire. "What did you do with the Cherokee all those years?"

"Farm, mostly," Reeves said. "And I don't mind saying I was terrible at it for sure."

"So how did you wind up a marshal for Judge Parker?" Dix said.

"Back in seventy-five, President Grant appointed Parker as territorial judge with orders to clean up Fort Smith," Reeves said. "He needed men who knew the Nation. I was sick of farming anyway and I'm a much better lawman than with a plow."

"Me too," Dix said. He stirred the pot. "Grab a hunk of bread, stew's ready."

Reeves picked up a plate and Dix filled it with a ladle.

"You a married man?" Reeves said.

"For the second time," Dix said. "My first wife died in Denver some six years ago. You?"

"Married Nellie in sixty-four," Reeves said. "We got seven children. So far. You got any kids?"

"Not yet," Dix said. "I'm working on buying a ranch. Maybe then."

"Pretty good stew," Reeves said. "I'm gonna sleep like a baby."

Chapter Twenty-Eight

"That was an excellent supper, Mrs. Dix," Newhouser said. "And the apple pie was delicious."

"Thank you, Mr. Newhouser," Trixie said. "Would you like more coffee?"

"I would, but let's go to the den," Newhouser said.

"The dishes can wait, Trixie," Pickford said.

They went to the den where a series of maps were laid out on the reading table.

"I brought these maps with me," Newhouser said. "These are association maps that show available land in various states. Have you given any thought to where you and your husband wish to buy land?"

"We talked about Montana and Wyoming," Trixie said.

"If you look at Montana you will see literally millions of acres of land for sale," Newhouser said. "I could be described as a cattleman's paradise, except for one thing. The long hard winters. Many start-up ranches never made it through the first winter."

"Wyoming?' Trixie said.

"Just as cold, but far less rainfall in much of the state," Newhouser said. "The problem with both for a new rancher is losing cattle over the winter. Lose too many and you'll never make it a second year."

"Dix spoke of that problem," Trixie said. "He said we need contingency money for just that reason."

"And he is right," Newhouser said. "If you lose even half your cattle the first winter, it could be devastating without contingency money to see you through the second year."

"What are some other places?" Trixie said.

"There are ranches in Arizona and Nebraska, but Arizona is very dry and water is a problem," Newhouser said. "Nebraska is more suited to farming. Corn, mostly. Since Chisum has moved to New Mexico, any ranch you might build will be an afterthought. Have you thought about Nevada?"

"Nevada?" Trixie said.

"South of Carson City is excellent land for ranching," Newhouser said. "And a much gentler climate. Mild winters with only about ten inches of snow annually."

"What does an acre go for in Nevada?" Pickford said.

"Oh, you should be able to get ten thousand acres for twenty thousand dollars," Newhouser said. "Possibly less."

"That's what Dix figured," Trixie said.

"You'll need money for a house, barn, corral and a bunkhouse," Newhouser said. "Five hundred head of cattle to start and maybe four cowboys. You'll need fifty-thousand-dollars that first year."

"That's also what Dix figured," Trixie said. "When can we see the land?"

"When will your husband be back?" Newhouser said.

"A month," Trixie said.

"As soon as he's back, we'll make arrangements," Newhouser said.

"Thank you, Mr. Newhouser," Trixie said. "And now I better tackle those dishes."

Pickford always liked to read before going to bed. He generally sat in his comfortable, leather chair in his study and read for one hour.

Trixie knocked on the door, opened it and brought Pickford a small glass of brandy.

"Thank you," Pickford said. "Please sit for a minute."

Trixie took a seat on the sofa.

"I was thinking of taking a small vacation," Pickford said. "I was wondering if you wouldn't mind if I went with you to Nevada to see the land when you go."

"Of course not, Judge," Trixie said. "We'd be happy to have you go with us."

"There is so much of this country I haven't seen," Pickford said. "I thought it would be a nice trip."

"We'll go as soon as Dix comes home," Trixie said. "What would you like for breakfast?"

Chapter Twenty-Nine

"We'll be in the village in about an hour," Reeves said.

"They picked us up when?" Dix said.

"Oh, two hours ago," Reeves said. "They know it's me. They already sent riders back to inform the village."

"If I was alone?"

"You'd either be escorted or be dead," Reeves said. "Since you know Waya, you'd probably be alright."

They rode for another fifty minutes until they reached the village, where Dix was surprised by what he saw.

Dozens of cabins lined a wide street. Dozens more were under construction. There were wagons of lumber, tools and kegs of nails. There were two well pumps and a police station.

There were still teepees, but not as many as Dix expected to find.

"What's happened here?" Dix said.

"Judge Parker said he'll be damned if the Nation under his care will go without," Reeves said. "He sent the Army Corps of engineers to teach home construction and got the Bureau of Indian Affairs to supply the necessary lumber and tools."

They dismounted at the police station. "They have thirty officers so far, all members of the five tribes," Reeves said.

"Is that a school?" Dix said.

"Yes. Come on, let's go in," Reeves said.

Reeves and Dix entered the police station and Dix got another surprise when Waya, wearing the police chief's badge, stood up from behind a desk.

"When did this happen?" Dix said.

Reeves grinned. "Three months ago, Judge Parker appointed Waya Chief of Reservation Police," he said.

Waya looked at Dix. "I did not expect to see you so soon," Waya said.

"Is that coffee I smell?" Reeves said.

"Lat's take a cup to the porch and you can tell me why you are here," Waya said.

Reeves filled three cups and they went to the porch where there were four rocking chairs. They sat and Dix rolled a cigarette and told Waya about Stephen Richards.

"This man sounds like he kills for sport," Waya said.

"Worse," Dix said. "For pleasure."

"And he is here in the mountains?" Waya said.

"That's the report we have," Dix said.

"Sleep here tonight," Waya said. "Myself and five of my police will go with you to track him down."

"I saw a dozen rifles inside in a rack, but no pistols," Dix said.

"The Judge wants to make sure they have proper training before he'll approve the expense for handguns for the police," Reeves said.

"The Chief of Police should have a sidearm," Dix said. He stood and went down to his horse, opened the saddlebag and removed a new Colt and black holster and brought it to Waya.

"For the Chief of Police," Dix said.

Waya stood up and removed the Colt from the holster. "This is a fine gun," he said.

"The best," Reeves said.

"Wear it with honor," Dix said.

"Now, what's a man got to do to get some food around here," Reeves said.

Waya shared his personal cabin with Dix and Reeves for dinner. Two Cherokee women served a full meal of meat and bread and coffee. Alcohol of any kind was forbidden by Judge Parker, but also by tribal law.

"I have to admit the cabin has certain advantages over the teepee in the winter months," Ways said. "Especially the wood stove."

"Where will we start in the morning?" Dix said.

"With my men," Waya said. "If he is out there, they will know."

"I expect we'll be up before the sun," Reeves said. "We best get some sleep."

CHAPTER THIRTY

After breakfast, well before the sun rose, Waya, Dix and Reeves met five of Waya's officers in front of the police station. The five officers were armed with Winchester rifles and carried their own supplies and water. They all noticed Waya's Colt and holster, but didn't speak of it.

"A hunting party reported a white man living like an animal thirty of your miles to the west," Waya said.

"Like an animal?" Dix said.

"In a cave like a bear or a wolf," Waya said.

"Well, the only way to know if it's Richards, the only way to know for sure is to go find him," Dix said.

Waya, Dix and Reeves rode in front of Waya's five officers as the left the village. They rode for an hour before the sun finally rose and day broke.

"These mountains cover a lot of territory," Reeves said when they paused for Waya and two of his men to scout ahead for a while. "Near fifty-thousand square miles."

Dix built a fire and made a pot of coffee. "Richards may be off in the head, but he's not stupid," Dix said. "He'll want to be near game and water if he's to survive and he wants to survive long enough for the law to forget about him, so he can come down and continue killing."

Waya and his two men returned. Everybody had a cup of coffee.

"This man, he is living off the land," Waya said. "He'll be high and near water."

"About what I figure," Dix said.

"My men will break up and scout to the north," Waya said. "We will continue west. Whoever finds his trail first will send up smoke and wait for the others to arrive."

After the Judge left for the courthouse, Trixie cleaned up the kitchen, did some housework and laundry, then changed and left to do some errands.

She walked to the market where the Judge had an account and placed a large order that would be delivered after four o'clock. Then she went to the post office to pick up his personal mail. The Judge's professional mail went to the courthouse.

Mixed in with the personal mail was a

telegram from Dix addressed to her. She couldn't wait to get home to read it, so she entered a small café, ordered a coffee and tore open the envelope.

Dix sent the telegram from Fort Smith, Arkansas. He didn't expect to be away from home more than a month, loved her, missed her and hoped she was moving forward with searching for their land.

She tucked the telegram into her drawstring purse and was about to leave when Angel entered the café and rushed to the table. Trixie stood and the two women hugged.

"What are you doing here?" Angel said.

"Running errands," Trixie said. "You?"

"Picking up the mail for the saloon," Angel said. "I sometimes come here for coffee and to kill some time before heading back."

They sat and ordered coffee.

Angel looked at Trixie's ring. "I see you married Dix," she said.

Trixie looked at her ring. "I did," she said.

"He must be one hell of a hard man to kill," Angel said. "Where is he?"

"Working," Trixie said.

"That's right, he's some kind of bounty hunter," Angel said.

"Federal Warrant Officer," Trixie said.

"He's away serving warrants for Judge Pickford."

"Where are you staying while he's away?' Angel said.

"I work for the Judge now," Trixie said. "We live there until we get our ranch."

"Sounds like you're doing well," Angel said. "I'm very happy for you."

"Angel, there is a life outside the saloon," Trixie said. "It's time you made a life of your own."

"Someday maybe I'll find it," Angel said.

"Let's have coffee again soon," Trixie said.

"Let's," Angel said.

Late in the afternoon, Dix, Reeves and Waya stopped to make camp. They had traveled a good forty miles and their horses needed rest and grain.

Dix made a fire for supper. Waya kept his eyes roaming the mountains. Before Dix got supper started, Waya pointed and said, "There."

To the north, smoke signals filled the sky.

Waya took his blanket, covered the fire and sent a message back to his men.

"What did you say?" Dix said.

"To wait for us in the morning," Waya said.

"Let's get supper going," Dix said.

■ ■ ■ ■

After supper, Dix, Reeves and Waya got into their bedrolls and watched the night sky. Millions of stars were visible. The moon wasn't up, the fire was out, their night vision wasn't obstructed.

"That bright star there, what do you call it?" Waya said.

"Venus," Dix said. "Named for an ancient goddess of love and beauty by a people called the Romans."

"Venus," Waya said.

"It's a planet and not a star," Dix said.

"What's the difference?" Waya said.

"When we get back to Fort Smith, I'll have a book about it sent to you," Dix said.

"There is an entire book about it?" Waya said.

"It's . . . I'll send you a book," Dix said.

Chapter Thirty-One

After a quick breakfast, Dix, Reeves and Waya rode north about ten miles where they met up with Waya's five officers.

There was the remains of the gut sack from a deer and a campsite.

"Five days ago at least," Waya said.

"He's close,' Dix said.

"He's near water," Waya said. "In the mountains north of here."

One of Waya's officers spoke to him in Cherokee.

"The waterfalls," Reeves said.

Waya nodded. "We could reach it by nightfall," he said.

At breakfast, Pickford told Trixie he was bringing Newhouser to dinner because he did some research on land in Nevada.

She made a special trip to the market for three small hens and roasted them in the oven with potatoes and carrots. She backed a cornbread to go with dinner and a blueberry pie for dessert.

"I'll make fresh whip cream with the pie and coffee," Trixie said.

"Judge, any chance I can steal her away from you?" Newhouser said.

"Now, Tom, I don't think your wife would tolerate having so pretty a woman in your employ," Pickford said.

"Mr. Newhouser, what information do you have about the land in Nevada?" Trixie said.

"Ten-thousand acres ten miles southeast of Carson City, for a dollar-seventy-five an acre," Newhouser said. "Governor Blasdell wants Nevada to rival Texas, New Mexico and Wyoming as cattle country and in order to do so he has to offer to sell land at a cheaper price. Carson City is a small town at the moment, but it's growing and Blasdell is counting on cattle to grow the entire state."

Pickford looked at Trixie. "We should take that vacation we spoke about and go take a look," he said. "It's only two days by train and I can use a rest from court."

"Go without telling Dix?" Trixie said.

"I'm sure he'd approve," Pickford said.

"I'd like to go and see this land myself," Newhouser said. "As head of the Stock

Growers Association, I should know what the land looks like I'm advising ranchers on."

"I'll make arrangements tomorrow," Pickford said.

From a height of two-thousand-feet, Dix used his binoculars to look down on the waterfall flowing from the mountain opposite him.

Waya had the binoculars Dix gave him six months ago and also looked down on the waterfalls.

"There is a horse on shore beside the creek running off the waterfall," Dix said. "Look behind the waterfall. I see what looks like a cave."

"How did he know about this place?" Waya said.

"I'll be sure to ask him that right after I handcuff him," Dix said.

Reeves looked up at the sky. "Be dark in thirty minutes," he said. "Let's make camp and figure out a plan."

They pulled back far enough from the edge of the cliff so that a campfire couldn't be seen from below and made camp.

Dix made a pot of coffee and while a supper of beef stew cooked in a pot, they discussed a plan.

"Can't rush him behind that waterfalls," Reeves said. "We don't know what he's armed with in that cave and we don't want anybody shot."

"We'll draw him out of the cave," Dix said.

"How?" Reeves said.

Trixie brought a glass of brandy to Pickford, who was reading in his study.

"Thank you, dear," he said. "Please sit for moment."

Trixie took a seat on the leather sofa.

"Don't be apprehensive about Nevada," Dix said. "Opportunities missed are opportunities lost forever. And besides, a little time away from my court room will do me some good."

"I wish he would telegraph us so I could tell him," Trixie said.

"He'll wire after the first job, before he starts the second," Pickford said. "We owe it to him to at least take a look."

Trixie nodded. "How long will we be gone?"

"Five days, possibly six," Pickford said.

"I better go pack," Trixie said. "And get some sleep."

Chapter Thirty-Two

They waited until they saw smoke rising from the cave behind the waterfalls. There was a wide ledge from the cave to the ground to the right of the falls where a man could enter and exit the cave without getting soaked.

Three of Waya's officers approached Richards' horse and lassoed him around the neck and the horse fought back, kicking and snorting.

Waya and Reeves hid behind some rocks about twenty feet away and waited.

"What's going on out there?" Richards said from inside the cave. "What's got you rattled you stupid animal?"

Richards appeared on the ledge, armed with a plains rifle and a hatchet in his belt. He saw the three officers with his horse. "You bloody savages,": he yelled and rushed toward them.

Directly above, on some rocks, Dix waited

with his rope. As Richards stepped forward, Dix dropped the rope around Richards' neck and pulled tightly. Richards dropped his plains rifle and Dix yanked hard on the rope.

Reeves and Waya walked to Richards, Reeves took out his handcuffs.

"Ya suns a bitches," Richards said. "Ya stinking cowards."

"Shut up," Reeves said.

"Fight me fair, ya miserable cowards," Richards said.

Dix released the rope and dropped down to the ground. Richards removed the rope and tossed it away. "What you want me for?" Richards said.

"Murder," Dix said.

Richards had a second knife hidden in the small of his back. He pulled it and Dix kicked Richards in the groin. As Richards doubled over, Dix kneed Richards in the chin with his right knee and as Richards straightened up, Dix knocked him unconscious with a right hook to the jaw.

"Bass, cuff him," Dix said.

As Reeves handcuffed Richards, Dix and Waya walked along the ledge and entered the cave.

"Oh, Jesus Christ," Dix said.

Hanging upside down from a rope tied to

the roof of the cave was a dead man, bleeding out.

Waya looked at Dix. "I don't understand," Waya said.

Dix sighed heavily. "Food," he said and walked out of the cave.

Waya stared at the hanging body with a look of disgust on his face.

After burying the body of the unknown man, Waya led the way back. Richards was tied to the saddle and rode between Reeves and Dix.

Richards seemed untroubled and actually started to sing. "Camp town races sing a song, doo daa, doo daa," he sang.

"Shut up," Dix said.

Richards quieted down and then started whistling.

"Man's crazy," Reeves said.

"As a bedbug," Dix said.

Trixie exited the post office just as Angel was walking up the steps.

"Trixie" Angel said. "Morning," Trixie said.

"Wait for me," Angel said. "We'll go for coffee."

Ten minutes later, Trixie and Angel were having coffee at the small café.

"How are things going?" Angel said.

"Well, Dix is still away, but I'm going to Nevada with the judge to look at some land," Trixie said.

"For the ranch?"

Trixie nodded. "Ten-thousand acres," she said.

"That's a lot of land," Angel said.

"It takes a lot to raise cattle, I suppose," Trixie said.

"How much does that cost?"

"Around twenty-thousand," Trixie said. "But that's just for the land. Dix figures we'll need around fifty-thousand for everything."

"Wow," Angel said. "Well, good luck, honey."

"See you when I get back," Trixie said.

As they ate supper around a campfire, Richards started singing again. Carry me Back to old Virginny.

"Shut up, Richards," Dix said. "For the last time."

"It's a long way to Nebraska," Richards said. "Turn your back on me and I'll chop you to bits."

"You sleep tied to a tree tonight, with a gag in your mouth," Dix said. "And if you open your mouth one more time, I tie a rope around your neck to the tree and you'll sleep standing up."

"I'll gut you like a fish and chop your head off," Richards said. "Ya sum bitch."

Dix drew his Colt and smacked Richards in the head, knocking him unconscious.

"If you hadn't, I would have," Reeves said.

"Pass the bread," Waya said.

Chapter Thirty-Three

Trixie, Pickford and Newhouser had lunch in the dining car of the westbound train to Carson City.

Trixie found the ride exciting and terrifying at the same time. Exciting because she hadn't been on a train but once or twice in her life and terrifying because she was going to look at land she had no right to think of buying without Dix by her side. She knew nothing about land, cattle and it was his money and every nickel hard earned with his life the

Pickford sensed her tension.

"Relax, Trixie," Pickford said. "We're simply taking a pleasant, fact finding trip to the west on behalf of Dix. That's all."

"I feel so . . . hesitant," Trixie said.

"Of course," Pickford said. "This is a big step in your life. In anybody's life."

"Mrs. Dix, I have never met your husband, but I would be willing to bet he will love the country we are going to see," New-houser said.

"I certainly hope so," Trixie said.

Judge Parker looked at Dix and Bass Reeves as they stood before him in his chambers. "You men look like you could use a drink," he said. "Bass, the globe."

Reeves went to the large globe against the wall and opened the top half, revealing a bar with glasses. He poured two small drinks of bourbon and gave one to Dix.

"I can have a marshal transport Richards to Lincoln for trial," Parker said.

Dix took a sip of his drink. "I would appreciate that, Judge," he said. "I have another warrant to serve in Missouri."

"Will you be staying the night in Fort Smith?" Parker said.

"At the hotel," Dix said. "Right now, I need a shave and a bath, a steak and about ten hours sleep.'

"I'd say you earned all four," Parker said.

Trixie wasn't prepared for the pleasant, little town of Carson City. As the capital of Nevada, she was expecting something more along the lines of Washington, but it was anything but.

Named foe Kit Carson, Carson City was

in the Eagle Valley and the surrounding mountains in the distance were lush and green.

"First stop is the hotel," Pickford said. "I wired ahead."

The Carson City Hotel was three-stories high with sixteen rooms. Trixie, Pickford and Newhouser had rooms on the second floor.

After checking into their rooms and freshening up a bit, they met in the lobby and walked over to City Hall where the land office was located.

After introducing themselves to the clerk, Newhouser requested maps of land for sale. They studied the maps and looked at acres abutting the Carson River.

"We'd like to see this land here that sits near the Carson River," Newhouser said.

"Good land for a ranch," the clerk said.

"That's the idea," Newhouser said.

"It's too late in the day to ride out there," the clerk said. "But if you meet me here at ten tomorrow morning, I'll ride you over."

"That would be perfect," Newhouser said.

Dix grabbed a shave and a bath and had his dirty laundry sent out to be washed. Then he sent a telegram home and took a cup of coffee on the porch of the hotel. He rolled and lit a cigarette and was surprised to see Bass Reeves come walking to the hotel porch.

"Leaving tomorrow?" Reeves said.

"Like I told the judge, I need to get to Missouri," Dix said.

"If you're so inclined, my misses would like you to come to dinner tonight," Reeves said.

"I'd be pleased," Dix said.

"You're not eating," Pickford said. He, Trixie and Newhouser were having dinner at a small restaurant on Main Street.

"I was thinking about Dix," Trixie said.

"Believe me, he's fine," Pickford said. "If ever a man could take care of himself it's him."

"I know you're probably right, but I can't help worrying about him," Trixie said.

"Tomorrow, after we see the land, I'm sure you'll feel a great deal better," Pickford said. "Tonight, eat your dinner. Judge's orders."

Trixie nodded and picked up her fork."

Bass Reeves lived in a modest house on a side street a block from the courthouse. The front yard was green grass and a flower garden.

"All these homes are occupied by marshals

of the court," Reeves said. "Come inside and meet my wife and kids."

Reeves' wife was named Nettie and like Reeves, she was born a slave. She was around Reeves' age and a polite, soft-spoken woman with an easy smile. Their seven children were polite and only spoke when spoken to, something Reeves drilled into them the moment they learned to talk.

Nettie prepared a large turkey with all the fixings and Reeves did the honors of slicing the bird.

Dessert was a fresh apple pie with coffee and milk for the children.

After dinner, Dix and Reeves took coffee on the porch. Dix rolled a cigarette and lit it with a wood match.

"You've a fine family, Bass," Dix said. "And Nettie is a fine lady."

"She is that, but she doesn't mind me being gone for long stretches," Reeves said. "She thinks seven kids is enough."

"And you don't" Dix said.

"I'm shooting for an even dozen," Reeves said. "As the good book says, be fruitful and multiple."

Dix grinned. "Yeah, but it isn't you carrying the fruit around for nine months."

Reeves looked at Dix and then burst into laughter.

Dix stood up. "Be seeing you, Marshal Reeves," he said.

Trixie couldn't sleep and went to the window for some fresh air. The street below was quiet and dark and the cool breeze coming in was refreshing.

She filled the wash basin with water from the pitcher and splashed some on her face. The truth was that she was not just worried about Dix, but that she felt unworthy of all the good things happening to her.

Six months ago, she was a Saloon girl in a Washington saloon. Now she was married and looking at land for a ranch her husband wanted to start. She loved Dix and he loved her and maybe that was enough to erase her past, but she carried a fear around inside her that she kept from telling him.

She worried that some man from the saloon would recognize her on the street and Dix would either kill the man, or regret marrying her.

Either would rip her apart.

She needed to sleep and returned to bed. Tomorrow would be a big day and she needed her wits about her.

After much tossing and turning, Trixie finally fell into a deep sleep and didn't stir until the sun shining through the window hit her in the eyes.

Chapter Thirty-Four

The ten o'clock train was scheduled to arrive in Saint Louis at six pm. Dix skipped breakfast after so heavy a meal at Reeves' house the night before and waited until one o'clock to eat lunch in the dining car.

He read the file on the Bender Family again and studied the photograph. The chances are they stayed together as a family after resettling along the Mississippi River.

If they were even still at the Mississippi River and if they were there to begin with. The reports were sketchy at best that the family had fled and resettled along the river and the information was now months old.

After lunch, at a water stop, Dix got off to stretch his legs for a few minutes. He rolled and smoked a cigarette. Other passengers also got off to stretch. He watched the engineer and his shoveler load water.

As soon as he reached Saint Louis, he would send another telegram to Trixie to let her know where he was.

Pickford rented a large buggy for the ride to see the land. The clerk had his maps and coordinates and the ride took just over an hour.

"Here we are," the clerk said and stopped the buggy near the Carson River.

Trixie, Pickford and Newhouser stood in tall grass beside the river.

"This is beautiful," Trixie said.

"A tributary of the Carson River runs straight through this property," the clerk said. "So you'd have good water."

"How much land is ten thousand acres?" Trixie said.

"Fifteen square miles," the clerk said. "But I must caution you, this land could sell tomorrow."

"No it won't," Pickford said. "I'm writing a check right now for one-thousand-dollars as a down payment."

"Judge, you . . ." Trixie said.

"I can and Dix would agree with me," Pickford said. "A paradise like this could be gone tomorrow."

"He's right, Mrs. Dix," Newhouser. "This land is a cattleman's paradise."

"Let's take a ride over to the tributary," the clerk said. "It's a good spot for a house."

■ ■ ■ ■

Dix stepped off the train in Saint Louis at six-fifteen in the evening. He walked his horse from the station to a hotel away from the main hub of the massive city and boarded his horse at a nearby livery.

After checking in, Dix sent a telegram home, then ordered a shave and a bath. The hotel restaurant was open late and he grabbed a steak around eight o'clock.

He wanted to wrap this job up quickly and get home to Trixie. He tried not to think about her while he was working, the distraction could be fatal, but he allowed himself the luxury tonight and tomorrow would push her out of his mind.

He wanted a couple of kids, not seven like Bass Reeves, but maybe two. He never discussed it with Trixie, so he didn't know how she felt about it, but he would breach the subject when he got home.

After dinner, he turned in early. Tomorrow would be a hard day in the saddle.

"It is some beautiful land," Trixie said.

"Some of the best I've ever seen," Newhouser said.

"Judge, what if Dix doesn't like it?" Trixie said.

"They will return my check," Pickford said. "But I am one hundred percent certain he will love it."

"I agree," Newhouser said. "Now, it's getting late, so let's order some supper."

Chapter Thirty-Five

After breakfast, Dix rode out of Saint Louis and followed the Mississippi River. He had the feeling the world hadn't heard the last of the Bender family. Finding them shouldn't be too difficult a task, they tended to leave a trail of dead bodies wherever they went.

Provided they didn't change their habits, which he doubted very much. It was reported they murdered twenty-one guests at their inn, so suddenly changing into model citizens was highly unlikely.

Dix rode thirty-five miles before dark. He saw freight wagons, farmers, sodbusters and some small outposts along the river, but nothing that resembled the Bender family.

Close to dark, he made camp near to the river and fixed supper. Afterward, he didn't bother to tie up or hobble his horse. There was too much sweet grass to feast on and if anybody tried to steal him in the night, the horse would simply stomp them.

In the morning, after a light breakfast, Dix continued on. After ten miles or so, he came to an outpost. Farmers needed a place to shop and trade without having to ride fifty miles into Saint Louis every time they ran low on coffee.

A dozen wagons were parked out front when Dix dismounted and tied his horse to a post. He didn't really need anything, but he bought some extra supplies in case he didn't see another town for a while.

As he left the outpost and walked to his horse, he spotted a tall man who seemed familiar. The man drove a wagon, parked and went into the outpost.

Dix put his supplies into his saddlebags and took out the photograph of the Bender family.

The man from the wagon was one of the Bender sons, of which there were two and two daughters.

Dix went up to the porch of the outpost, sat in a chair and rolled and lit a cigarette and waited.

Fifteen minutes later, the Bender son came out with a sack full of supplies and went to his wagon.

Dix rolled and smoked another cigarette and gave the wagon a decent head start before mounting up and following the wagon tracks. It was an easy follow. The heavy wagon left deep tracks that a child could follow.

About ten miles from the outpost, Dix spotted a river-raft crossing. That's where the wagon tracks headed. From a distance, Dix used his binoculars for a closer look. There was a fairly large cabin, with a corral and small barn. The large raft was anchored to shore by ropes that went under water across the river and were anchored on the other side to heavy posts. A wood sign read, *River Crossing One Dollar Fifty cents. Crossing every two hours until sunset.*

Mother and two daughters were in chairs on the porch. Father and two sons were at the raft, tightening ropes.

All six matched the six in the photograph.

Dix put the binoculars away and rode to the river crossing and dismounted near the raft. "Afternoon. When is the next crossing?' Dix said.

"Hour," the father said.

"Why can't I cross now?" Dix said. "I'll pay extra for the privilege."

"People round here know the schedule," father said. "They'll show up a few minutes before it time to cross. Why don't you go on the porch and wait in the shade. My misses will give you a glass of lemonade."

The two sons eyed Dix.

"Alright," Dix said. He walked his horse to the porch and loosely tied his horse to the porch railing. "Ma'am," he said.

"Come on up and have a cool glass of lemonade," Mother said.

"Thank you kindly," Dix said. He went up to the porch where mother pouted a glass of lemonade for Dix and handed it to him.

"Thank you kindly, ma'am,: Dix said. He took a sip of lemonade and said, "Excellent. Thank you."

The two daughters were around eighteen and twenty, both pretty girls. They both smiled at Dix.

"We got a critter in the barn," daughter one said.

"A critter?" Dix said. "What kind of critter?"

"Don't know," daughter two said.

"Maybe you can tell us what it is," daughter one said.

"That's a good idea, honey," mother said. "Take him to the barn and show him the critter."

The two daughters stood up. "Come see," daughter one said.

"Alright," Dix said.

"This way," daughter two said.

Dix and the two daughters left the porch and walked to the barn.

"We got it penned up, but we don't know what it is," daughter one said.

"Well, let's have a look," ix said.

As they entered the barn, both daughters pulled long, hunting knives from pockets on their skirts.

"It's right over there in that stall," daughter one said.

Dix said, "Where? That one?" and drew his Colt a second before both daughters attacked with their knives. He shot them both, then ran out the back door and around to the front of the barn as father and two sons ran to the open door, all three armed with long knives.

Dix stepped out in front of the father and two sons. "You're under arrest by a federal warrant," Dix said.

"Screw you," the father said. He and the two sons charged Dix with knives raised.

"Suit yourself," Dix said and shot the three of them dead.

As he reloaded the Colt, mother came running from the porch with a shotgun. "You kilt them," she screamed and cocked the shotgun. "And I'll kill you, ya sum bitch."

Dix shot her before she could fire the shotgun.

He loaded the bodies into the wagon and covered them with blankets from the cabin. Then he hitched the team, tethered his horse to the wagon and rode back to Saint Louis.

Trixie placed an order at the general store, then went to the post office for the mail. On the way out, she ran into Angel, who was picking up the mail for the saloon.

"Trixie, where have you been?" Angel said.

"Nevada," Trixie said.

"Let me get the mail and we'll go for coffee," Angel said.

Ten minutes later, Trixie and Angel were having coffee at the small café.

"So, what's in Nevada?" Angel said.

"Land," Trixie said. "I looked at ten-thousand acres for Dix."

"Ten . . . how much does that cost?" Angel said.

"Almost twenty-thousand-dollars."

"Dix has that kind of money?"

"At least twice that, but it's still not enough," Trixie said. "He wants to work one more year."

"I didn't realize a ranch was that expensive," Angel said.

"To do it right," Trixie said. "Listen, why don't you quit that place? You don't need to work there. Judge Pickford knows everybody in Washington. He could help get you a respectable job."

"When the time is right,: Angel said. "I will."

Chapter Thirty-Six

Trixie left Pickford's home at one o'clock to walk to the railroad depot to meet Dix, who was on the one-thirty train.

The train was on time and she picked him out of the crowd immediately due to his height. He was dressed in his black trail clothes and needed a shave and a bath and probably a hot meal.

She ran to him and he embraced her with a hug and kiss.

"Come on, I need to get my horse," Dix said.

They waited for the platform to clean, then went to the boxcar for Dix's horse. They walked him back to the Judge's house.

"What do you want first?" Trixie said. "A bath or a hot meal?"

"Is there a third option?" Dix said.

"Sure," Trixie said. "Shave and bath first. I'll get the hot water ready."

■ ■ ■ ■

Trixie waited until they finished up in the bedroom and dressed and went to the kitchen where she started dinner.

She made coffee and Dix took a chair at the table and rolled a cigarette.

At the oven, her back to Dix, Trixie said, "Dix, honey, I have something important to tell you."

"You're pregnant?" Dix said.

"What? No. Not that," Trixie said. "While you were away, The judge and I and the man in charge of the Stock Growers Association, Mr. Newhouser went to look at some land."

"The judge went to look at land?" Dix said. "Where?"

"Nevada," Trixie said. "It's near Carson City. It's the most beautiful country I've ever seen. The judge put a deposit on it, so nobody can buy it before you see it."

"He did that?" Dix said.

"Yes. So, do you want to see it or not?" Trixie said.

"Did you get a price?" Dix said.

"A dollar-seventy-five an acre," Trixie said. "The lot is ten-thousand acres."

Dix nodded as he sipped coffee. "That's

below what I expected," he said.

"The governor of Nevada said he wants to make Nevada real cattle country," Trixie said. "It sits near the Carson River and a creek runs right through the property."

"When can we see it?" Dix said.

"Did you finish the Richards and Bender business?" Pickford said as he entered the kitchen.

"Richards is headed to the gallows in Nebraska and the Bender family was scheduled for boot hill," Dix said.

Trixie looked at Dix. She knew not to ask. He would talk about it if he wanted to.

"Stop by my chambers in the morning for payment, then take Trixie west to Nevada," Pickford said. "The pending warrants can wait a week or so."

"Trixie?" Dix said.

"Let's do," Trixie said.

"Good," Pickford said. "Now, what's for dinner?"

After dinner, while Trixie tidied up the kitchen Dix and Pickford took coffee on the front porch.

"What happened with Richards?" Pickford said.

"He was hiding in a cave in the eastern Ozarks," Dix said. "A marshal from Judge

Parker's court helped me track him, along with a Cherokee chief named Waya. He didn't put up much of a fight. I expect he'll be hung pretty quickly."

"And the Bender family?"

"A crazier bunch you never did see," Dix said. "They murdered the family who ran a river crossing on the Mississippi and took their place. If someone came along they thought worth robbing, the two daughters would entice him into the barn where he'd be stabbed to death."

"You killed them all?" Pickford said.

"No choice," Dix said.

"No matter," Pickford said. "Tomorrow, pick up the bounty, then head to Nevada and see that land. It's a prize, Dix. I wouldn't let it slip through your hands."

Almost asleep, Dix woke up when Trixie gently nudged him and said, "Dix, honey, are you still awake?"

"I am now," Dix said.

"When you asked tonight if I was pregnant, were you hoping I said yes?" Trixie said.

"In a way," Dix said.

"We can talk about it on the train," Trixie said.

"Okay," Dix said and fell asleep.

Chapter Thirty-Seven

Trixie had a map of the area south of Carson City. She pointed to the land abutting the Carson River. "This creek runs from the river right through the property," Trixie said and traced the creek with her finger. "And Carson City is just ten miles away, so getting supplies won't be difficult."

They were in the dining car, having coffee after lunch.

Dix smoked a cigarette as he studied the map. "Seventeen thousand-five-hundred leaves twenty-eight-thousand left," he said. "It's not enough to build a house, barn, corral, bunkhouse, buy stock and horses. I have to keep working another year at least."

"Dix, I've learned a few things from the judge," Trixie said. "There is such a thing as a mortgage."

"I know," Dix said. "But a bank doesn't care if you fail and go broke, they expect to be paid on time or you lose everything. One more year is what we need and we're free and clear of it all. We'll never be broke as long as we own land."

Trixie took a sip of her coffee, set the cup down and said, "Now about that other thing."

"What other thing?" Dix said.

"Children."

"Oh that other thing," Dix said.

"I would like two," Trixie said. "One of each."

"Boys are more use on a ranch," Dix said.

"Then I'll have three," Trixie said. "Or as many as it takes to get you two sons."

"Then we better build a big house," Dix said.

"Let's get started right now," Trixie said.

"Building a house?" Dix said.

"No, silly, stocking it with kids," Trixie said as she stood up and took Dix by the hand.

Dix gently shook Trixie awake. "Let's go, hon, we're in Carson City."

Trixie sat up in bed. "Give me ten minutes to wash up and get dressed," she said.

"The train won't leave for an hour," Dix said. "I'll bring you some coffee."

Dix left the sleeping car. Trixie filled a basin with water and washed her face. Then she applied a touch of makeup and brushed her hair. As she slipped into a dress, Dix returned with two cups of coffee. He set one on the dresser, then took a chair and rolled a cigarette.

As he watched Trixie dress, she smiled at him. “What?” he said.

“You,” Trixie said. “You’re the only man I’ve ever met who actually cared about what I thought or said.”

“Isn’t that what a husband is supposed to do?” Dix said.

“Supposed to and does are often not related,” Trixie said. “I’m ready.”

“We can have breakfast and then I’ll rent a buggy,” Dix said.

The clerk at the land office was free of appointments and he accompanied Dix and Trixie south of Carson City to look at the land.

The first stop was at the tributary of the Carson River that cut through the ten Thousand acres.

“Good water,” Dix said. “We could have a pump in the kitchen and another outside and one in the bunkhouse.”

Dix studied the maps the clerk brought with him. “At the moment, are there any other ranches nearby?”

"Twenty miles south in the Porter ranch," the clerk said and marked the spot on the map. Otherwise, not at the moment. However, I caution you that the governor is keen to make this area a cattlemen's dream, so land is going to sell quickly."

Dix looked at Trixie. "Yes or no?" he said.

"Yes," Trixie said.

"You heard my wife," Dix said. "Let's go back to town."

At the Carson City Bank, Dix made arrangements to have sixteen-thousand and five hundred dollars wired to the bank from Washington.

Then he and Trixie returned to the land office and filled out the paperwork to buy the land.

"I'll have the funds for you in the morning," Dix told the clerk.

"Congratulation, Mr. and Mrs. Dix, you are now land owners," the clerk said.

After leaving the clerk, Dix and Trixie walked around Carson City to get the feel of the town. It was small, but prosperous and growing and had a large schoolhouse and even a small library.

"Not a bad place to call home," Dix said. "Let's wire the judge and then grab some lunch.'

They found a small café on Front Street for lunch and ordered a light meal. "We need to find an architect," Dix said. "To design the house and bunkhouse for us."

"This is really happening, isn't it?" Trixie said.

"Starting today," Dix said.

"Where do we find an architect?" Trixie said.

Dix looked at his pocket watch. "Let's go see the clerk, he'll know," he said.

"We don't have an architect in town, not yet anyway," the clerk said. "But there is a firm in San Francisco that's used quite often here in town. I'll give you his card. Send him a wire."

The firm in San Francisco was named Riley and Farber. Dix and Trixie sent a telegram from the telegraph office, then told the operator to notify them at the hotel when there was a response.

Dix and Trixie were getting dressed when there was a soft knock on the door. "Yes?" Dix said.

"Telegram for you, sir," a man said from the hallway.

Dix opened the door and took the telegram. "Could you wait one moment," Dix said and closed the door.

Dix read the telegram and said, "It's from Riley and Farber. They would like to meet with us here in Carson City."

"When?" Trixie said.

"It's four hours by train," Dix said. "Tomorrow? Yes?"

"Yes," Trixie said.

Dix found a pencil and wrote the reply, then opened the door and handed it and five dollars to the messenger. "Get this off right away," Dix said.

"Very good," the messenger said.

Dix closed the door and looked at Trixie.

"All of a sudden I don't feel like getting dressed," Trixie said. "You?"

Chapter Thirty-Eight

Dix and Trixie waited for the eleven o'clock train from San Francisco to arrive. It was on time and as passengers exited the train, Dix held up a sign he made that read, Riley and Farber.

A man of average height, around fifty-years-old and wearing an expensive suit and carrying a briefcase spotted the sign and walked to Dix and Trixie.

"Mr. and Mrs. Dix, I'm John Farber,"

Dix shook his hand. "I have a buggy and thought you could see the land where we want to build our home," Dix said.

"That's the best way to get started," Faber said. "I always like to know the landscape I'm dealing with before anything else."

They rode to the land in the buggy. On the way, Farber took samples of his work out of his briefcase and showed them to Trixie. "These are beautiful photographs," she said.

"I document all the homes and buildings I design using a photographer named Richard Carr," Farber said. "I show them to potential clients to give them a feel for what is possible for their dreams."

They reached the creek by twelve-thirty.

"Well, let's take a look," Farber said.

"Mr. Farber, did you have breakfast this morning?" Trixie said.

"Actually, I didn't," Farber said.

"I took the liberty of packing a picnic lunch," Trixie said. "We can talk as we eat."

"That sounds like a very good idea," Farber said.

After spreading out a blanket, Dix brought a large picnic basket out from the rear of the buggy. It was loaded with fried chicken from town, with salad and a jug of cold lemonade and apple pie.

"I have to admit that this is a perfect spot to start a ranch," Farber said.

"What do you think of the location for a house, bunkhouse, corral and barn?" Dix said.

"This area here is relatively flat, which makes it easy to grade the land to build upon," Farber said. "Let's walk around and I'll make some sketches."

After eating lunch, Farber, Dix and Trixie walked the area where they wanted the house. "We'd like an indoor pump in the house and the bunkhouse and one pump outside," Dix said.

"How many rooms in the house?" Farber said.

"Four bedrooms, a den, kitchen, dining room, pantry and . . . ?" Dix looked at Trixie.

"Sewing room and a parlor," Trixie said. "And a nice front porch facing the sunset."

"The bunkhouse?" Farber said.

"Room for twelve bunks and a kitchen," Dix said. "The barn needs to be large enough for a dozen or more horses," Dix said.

Faber took some measurements and made some more sketches. "With this creek from the Carson River, it should be fairly easy to dig a well and run pipe," he said. "Now let's look at some styles. All ranch houses vary from the owner's particular taste.

"Dix and Trixie went through all the photographs and selected two and Dix said, "Can you somehow combine these two and make it original?"

"That's usually how this works," Farber said. "Let me take some final measurements and we can be on our way."

At the hotel,. Dix said, "What do you need

to get started?"

"A five hundred dollar deposit and I will send you six sets of sketches and blueprints for you to choose from," Farber said. "And an address for me to mail them to in about a month."

"The bank is closed, will you take cash?" Dix said.

"I'll write you a receipt," Farber said. "And if you could drive me to the train, I'd like to make the five o'clock back to San Francisco. I'd like to get started right away."

Dix and Trixie were walking to the hotel after supper at a café when Dix stopped suddenly and said, "Stay here."

"Why? What is . . . ?" Trixie said.

"Stay here," Dix said.

Dix walked into the street and approached the town sheriff from the right side. The sheriff was standing opposite two drunk men who were giving the sheriff a difficult time.

"Now boys, you know the rule about public intoxication," the sheriff said. "I want you to come along with me to jail and sleep it off."

"We ain't going nowhere, law dog," one of the men said. "Cept back into that saloon to finish our drinking."

"Come peacefully, boys," the sheriff said. "Sleep it off and I'll get you a nice breakfast in the morning."

Both men put their hands on their guns.

Dix stepped forward. "I wouldn't do that, boys," he said.

The two men looked at Dix. "Who is you?" one of them said.

"Federal Warrant Officer and you do as the sheriff says," Dix said.

"Federal what?" one of the men said.

"Warrant Officer and do as the sheriff says," Dix said.

"Or what?" the other man said.

"I'll kill the both of you where you stand," Dix said.

The two men stared at Dix. Dix drew his Colt and cocked it so fast they could barely see it.

"I won't ask again," Dix said.

"He isn't fooling fellows," the sheriff said. "Now why not sleep it off in a warm bunk and have a nice breakfast in the morning instead of spending the night on boot hill?"

The two men unbuckled their holsters and dropped them to the floor.

"Smart move," the sheriff said.

Dix holstered his Colt and as he walked back to Trixie, people on the street clapped.

Trixie took his arm. "I'm shaking like a

leaf," she said.

They continued walking to the hotel. "Would you really have killed those men?" Trixie said.

"Well, I wouldn't have let them kill a sheriff," Dix said.

They reached the hotel. "I think there's a reward waiting for you in our room for saving the sheriff's life," Trixie said.

Chapter Thirty-Nine

"We own the land an and an architect in San Francisco is drawing up blueprints for the house and the rest," Dix said. "I'll write you a check for the thousand you put down as a deposit."

"Are you ready to return to work?" Pickford said. "Lot's to be done."

"I'm ready," Dix said.

"Stop by my chambers in the morning," Pickford said. "And forget about writing me a check. I'll keep a thousand off your next bounty."

Dix rolled a cigarette and lit it with a wood match. They were on the front porch of Pickford's house. The street was quiet and dark, except for the street lanterns.

"I knew you would like that land in Nevada," Pickford said. "It's some of the best I've ever seen."

"Judge, we've known each other for a while now," Dix said.

"Close to seven years if memory serves," Pickford said.

"So let me ask you a personal question," Dix said. "How old are you?"

"Sixty. Why?"

"I was wondering when you figure to retire?" Dix said.

"Retire to what?" Pickford said. "An empty house and nothing to do except read and get fat."

"Carson City could use a good federal judge at the capital and the ranch isn't but an hour's ride by buggy," Dix said.

"I think you've been chasing outlaws too long," Pickford said.

"I'm serious, Judge," Dix said.

"You're a newly married man about to start a ranch, what would you want an old man like me hanging around?" Pickford said.

"It was Trixie who suggested it," Dix said. "And I think it's a fine idea."

"How much money do you have left?"

"Twenty-eight-thousand after the last batch. I'll need at least forty."

"That's another year," Pickford said. "We'll talk about it in a year."

"By then the house will be ready to move into," Dix said.

"A lot can happen in a year," Pickford

said. "Right now I suggest we go in to dinner before Trixie drops a flowerpot on our heads."

After dinner, Dix went to Pickford's stable behind the house to groom his horse. Trixie and Pickford took coffee at the kitchen table.

"Dix told me about your invitation to move to Carson City," Pickford said.

"Well, how about it?" Trixie said. "A fresh start for all of us."

"May I ask why this crazy idea came to you?" Pickford said.

"I see how hard you work," Trixie said. "Leaving at eight in the morning, coming home at seven and on weekends, you spend all your time reading those legal papers in your den. A change will do us all some good."

"You and Dix are just starting out together," Pickford said. "And I know nothing about living on a ranch."

"That makes two of us," Trixie said. "My father sold me for two-hundred-dollars when I was ten-years-old to a traveling pimp. You knew what I was and never sat in judgement on me. You're more of a father to me than my real one ever was. So, why not go with us and help get our feet wet in the ranching business?"

"I'll tell you what I told Dox," Pickford said. "Ask me again in a year."

Chapter Forty

Dix looked at the wanted poster of Will Langley. The reward was seven-thousand and five hundred dollars, dead or alive. The charge was murder.

"This one is a bad as they come," Pickford said. "A certified raciest if ever there was one. Hates Blacks and Mexicans and goes out of his way to kill them in cold blood. He's from Austin County, Texas. He's killed at least thirty men and women."

"Women?" Dix said.

"Several of his victim were freed slave women," Pickford said. "Like I said, as bad as they come. He left Texas a few years back, but returned and picked up his old ways."

"It says he was seen working as a sharecropper for a preacher named William R. Lay in east Texas," Dix said. "Is that the starting point?"

"It's all they have at the moment," Pickford said. "Go to Austin and assist the aid of the Texas Rangers in finding where the Lay farm is located. I imaging the Rangers will be very interested in locating him."

"I'll leave in the morning," Dix said.

"Use the Rangers on this one," Pickford said. "Killing is sport for this man. A sport he seems addicted to. Bring him in to hang, if possible."

"I will," Dix said.

"Go spend the day with your wife," Pickford said. "I imagine she won't be too thrilled at the idea of you leaving."

"No sir, she won't."

"Tomorrow?" Trixie said.

"The sooner I go, the quicker I return and with an additional seventy-five-hundred for our ranch," Dix said. "And while I'm away, when the blueprints arrive I'd like you to approve the one you like best."

"Without you here?"

"I trust your judgement," Dix said. "Now, how about some lunch?"

"I have to get the Judge's mail first," Trixie said.

Trixie and Dix left the post office. Trixie had an armload of mail. As they walked along the street, Dix said, "Let eat out for lunch."

"There's a little café on the next block," Trixie said.

Dix took Trixie's free arm. "Alright," he said.

They walked to the café, entered and found a vacant table. Trixie put the Judge's mail on the extra chair. "Does he always get so much mail?" Dix said.

"Usually more," Trixie said.

A waitress came to the table. They ordered the luncheon special of beef stew with break and coffee.

"I have to place an order at the market," Trixie said.

After lunch, they walked to the large market where Trixie placed the regular order with the manager. As they walked home, Trixie said, "There's Angel."

Angel was walking toward them on the same street. They stopped to chat for a few minutes.

"Trixie, honey, I never got the chance to thank Dix for what he did for helping us with Congressman Post," Angel said. "May I?"

Trixie nodded. Angel kissed Dix on the cheek.

Trixie said, "Did you think about quitting

the saloon like we talked about?"

"I did," Angel said. "Let's have coffee tomorrow and we'll talk. Right now I have to get the mail."

"Tomorrow," Trixie said.

Dix and Trixie continued walking home. "She's quitting the saloon?" Dix said.

"I hope so," Trixie said. "Now that you've had lunch, when we get home, how about some dessert?"

Chapter Forty-One

The train ride to Austin was scheduled for thirty-six hours. Dix boarded his horse in the boxcar and got a sleeper car for himself.

He had breakfast with Trixie and the Judge, then she walked with him to the train. It left on time at ten in the morning and Dix spent the better part of the morning and afternoon in his car, reading the reports on Will Langley.

Langley first murdered when he was just seventeen in 1867. He shot and killed three former slaves, who were just walking along a dirt road on the way to visit friends. After that, he and his brother-in-law embarked on a crime and killing spree together. They robbed settlers and murdered several more freed slaves.

Once he was identified, he escaped Texas by traveling north and joining the army in 1870. He deserted, was caught and imprisoned for four months. Upon his release, due to his outstanding marksmanship skills, he was assigned to regular hunting parties. On one hunting party, he deserted again and made his way back to Texas.

By 1873, Langley was back to his old tricks of murdering people. He was particularly hard on freed slaves and Mexicans and by 1875, he went into hiding again, reportedly living on his family's farm.

After that, he disappeared for several years until he was reported living as a sharecropper on the Reverend William R. Lay's farm, but when the county sheriff went to investigate, Lay told him Langley had wandered off to parts unknown.

Most likely Langley was insane, but as Dix knew, insane didn't mean stupid.

Stupid would be easier to catch.

Trixie met Angel at the café for a light lunch.

"So tell me about it? What happened?" Angel said.

"We bought the land," Trixie said. "Ten-thousand acres."

"Goodness. How much?"

"Seventeen-thousand, five hundred," Trixie said.

"The son of a gun really does have that kind of money," Angel said. "Who would have believed it."

"When I first met him, not me," Trixie said. "And believe me, every penny he has is hard earned."

"Where is he now?"

"Headed to Texas to track some outlaw," Trixie said. "I'm not sure how long he'll be gone."

"He's a special kind of man, Trixie. I saw it that night he took care of post," Angel said. "You're a very lucky woman."

"I know it and I'm grateful to whoever up there is looking out for me," Trixie said.

"So when do you move?"

"Lots to do first," Trixie said. "We have to approve the blueprints on the house and Dix wants to earn as much as he can before we go."

"I wish you only the best, honey," Angel said.

"Now let me ask you something," Trixie said. "Have you considered leaving the saloon and coming to work with me?"

"The Judge doesn't need two housekeepers," Angel said. "But when you and Dix head west, I'd be happy to take over for you."

"I'll settle for that," Trixie said. "Except that we're hoping he retires and comes with us."

"I swear, Trixie, if you don't beat all," Angel said.

After supper in the dining car, Dix retired to his sleeper car and read a book for several hours until he grew tired enough to sleep.

Over the years, Dix developed the habit of carrying a book to read to pass the time on long train rides. Although he read all different genres of books, the one he brought with him was a Jules Verne, science fiction novel titled Around the World in Eighty Days.

He read one hundred pages before growing sleepy enough to turn down the sheets and get some sleep.

After midnight, Trixie got out of bed and went to the kitchen to warm some milk on the woodstove. She was pouring a glass when Pickford startled her by entering the kitchen.

"Judge, you gave me a scare," Trixie said.

"I'm sorry," Pickford said. "I heard the noise and I knew you couldn't sleep."

"Would you like some of this warm milk?" Trixie said.

"I would. Thank you."

Trixie filled a second glass and they sat at the table. Pickford raised the flame on the table lantern, then took a sip.

"I'm awake because I miss Dix and am worried about him," Trixie said. "Why are you awake?"

"I'm awake because I have to sentence a man to hang tomorrow," Pickford said.

"Sometimes I forget how difficult it must be for you as a judge," Trixie said. "The decisions you have to make, the lives in your hands, it must be awful for you."

"At times, it weighs heavily, I admit," Pickford said. "But it's a job that needs doing or we have no society and if we have no society, we might as well be a pack of wolves."

Trixie sipped some warm milk. "Even wolves take time off to play," she said. "I remember this one time, after I'd been sold and was traveling across the plains in the wagon. They stopped to camp and I saw a pack of wolves playing in a field of wild flowers. They weren't bothering us, just nipping each other and playing like puppies."

"I'm sensing a message in there somewhere," Pickford said.

Trixie grinned. "Drink your milk," she said.

Chapter Forty-Two

Austin, the capital of Texas, was a prominent city of eleven-thousand residents. As Dix walked his horse from the railroad depot through the streets, it struck him that Austin was an eclectic mix of cowboy and socialite come together.

Socialite because it was home to the governor and cowboy because surrounding it were cattle ranches.

Austin sat on the banks of the Colorado River, which allowed it to grow rapidly as the railroad and ships allowed goods to be moved quickly.

Dix stopped at the Hotel Austin in the center of the city, registered for a room and livery for his horse. He ordered a shave and a bath, then dressed in clean clothes and left the room wearing his holster and Colt.

He walked to the Capital Building where the Texas Rangers were located across the street in a separate building.

After presenting his identification to a desk sergeant, Dix was escorted to the office of Captain Xavier J. Foxx.

Foxx, a native born Texan, was half Mexican and Half Irish. He was fifty-years-old, tall and stately and sported a pencil-thin moustache.

Foxx read Dix's identification and the warrant issued by Pickford. "Langley has been on our watch list for years," Foxx said. "We heard he was back in Texas, but haven't been able to figure out where."

"It was reported he's sharecropping on a farm owned by a Reverend Lay, a preacher," Dix said. "Langley wasn't there when a county sheriff went to investigate, but I'd like to talk to Lay myself."

"Which county?" Foxx said.

"Mason."

"That's a hundred miles northwest of here," Foxx said. He stood up from his desk and went to his office door, opened and said, "Sergeant, get me Sergeant Bauer right away."

Foxx closed the door and returned to his desk.

"Unfortunately, the train that passes through Macon County has already left for today and the next one isn't until ten tomorrow morning," Foxx said.

"Two hours on a train or three days in the saddle, I'll take the two hours," Dix said.

There was a knock on the door. It opened and Sergeant Bauer entered the office. "You sent for me, Captain?" he said.

"Come in and close the door," Foxx said.

Bauer closed the door and walked to the desk.

"Sergeant, this is Mr. Dix," Foxx said. "He is a Federal Warrant Officer sent by Washington with a warrant for the arrest of Will Langley."

"That one," Bauer said. "He's the worst of the worst."

"He was seen in Macon County not long ago, working as a sharecropper on a farm owned by . . . ?" Foxx said.

"Reverend Lay," Dix said. "The local sheriff got a tip Langley was there, but he was gone by the time he investigated."

"Take a ride tomorrow with Mr. Dix and see what you can find out," Foxx said.

"Yes sir," Bauer said.

"Sergeant, I'm at the Austin Hotel," Dix said. "Why not have dinner with me around seven and I'll fill you in on what I have."

"Seven at the Austin Hotel," Bauer said. "I'll be there."

Captain, where is the telegraph office?" Dix said. "I'd like to send a wire my wife."

■ ■ ■ ■

Trixie and Angel had coffee and pie at the café after picking up the mail.

"What kind of man is the Judge?" Angel said.

"A fine man," Trixie said. "One of the finest I've ever known. He never sits in judgement or looks down on me. Always kind and caring, it doesn't surprise me Dix is his friend."

"Sounds like the daddy you never really had," Angel said.

"Crazy as that sounds, it's true," Angel said. "That's how I've come to think of him these past months."

"That's good," Angel said. "That's really good."

"Well, I have to get back before the delivery man arrives with my order," Trixie said.

"Not a bad steak," Dix said.

"You're in Texas," Bauer said. "It's pretty much all we got. That and tequila."

Bauer had ordered two shot glasses of tequila and Dix took a small sip of his. "What's this made from?" he said.

"Some Mexican cactus plant," Bauer said. "So about this Longley?"

"He's the worst I've seen and I've seen some bad ones," Dix said. "He kills out of hate is the best I can figure. He especially hates freed slaves and Mexicans, although no one knows why. He's never shared his opinions."

"He's native born to Texas," Bauer said. "The war's been over fourteen years, but many folks down here still aren't over it yet. They see freed slaves walking around that they once called property and it breeds hate and resentment."

"And that gives him the right to go around killing them?" Dix said.

"In his mind it probably does," Bauer said. "When the war broke out, Texas had a population of six-hundred-thousand and a quarter of a million slaves. Men like Langley get all twisted up inside."

"Maybe so, but he killed his first man eight years before the war started," Dix said.

"Crazy in the head is all I can say," Bauer said. "With a heart full of hate. And I'll tell you something else. He's not the only one and that hate isn't going away anytime soon."

"A man's opinions are his own, but what Longley is doing goes beyond hate," Dix said.

"I can't argue that," Bauer said.

Finished with their steaks, Dix said, "Care for dessert? Dinner is on me."

"Believe I will," Bauer said.

Chapter Forty-Three

The train ride to Mason took just over two hours. The dining car was open and Dix and Bauer drank coffee to pass the time. Dix had a fresh tobacco pouch and papers and rolled two cigarettes and gave one to Bauer.

"I'm curious, Dix. Which side did you fight for in the war?" Bauer said.

"North. You?"

"Same."

"I served with Grant," Bauer said.

"You're a native Texan, aren't you?" Dix said.

"My family owned a large farm outside of San Antonio," Bauer said. "My daddy owned eighteen slaves. He treated them right, never had them whipped, always made sure they had the best food and a nice bunkhouse. But they were still property, like a wagon or a horse. Even let them have Sunday service in the bunkhouse."

"And you disagreed with you father?" Dix said.

"No, not at all," Bauer said. "I grew up with the slave mentality. Until I was eighteen and my family sent me to an agricultural college in Boston. That was in fifty-nine, I believe."

"So what happened?" Dix said.

"I couldn't believe my eyes at what I saw," Bauer said. "There were black men and women everywhere. Working, going to school, black kids playing with white kids, it was the most amazing thing I had ever seen. At the college, I had a black professor. His name was Jefferson and he was born a slave in Georgia. He escaped on the Underground Railroad and he knew more about farming than any man I ever met. Sometimes after class, I'd talk with him about his life as a slave. If any man had the right to be bitter and full of hate, it was him, but he wasn't. When the war broke out in sixty-one, I knew which side I stood on."

"But you came back to Texas?" Dix said.

Bauer grinned. "I don't like snow," he said.

The train slowed its speed.

"I do believe we're here," Bauer said.

"You're too late," Sheriff Hardy said. "Longley murdered Reverend Lay as the man sat milking a cow. He stole a horse and rode to Grayson County where he broke two of his friends out of jail. We captured one of them when he fell off a horse he was trying to steal."

"And you didn't think to notify the Rangers about all this?" Bauer said.

"And you're gonna do what if I had?" Hardy said.

"Sheriff, the man who fell off his horse, where is he now?" Dix said.

"Back in Grayson County lock-up, where else?" Hardy said.

Dix looked at Bauer. "Know where that is?"

"Yeah, another twelve hours on a train," Bauer said. "North."

"Sheriff, when is the next train north?" Dix said.

"Two o'clock," Hardy said.

"You know anyplace we can grab a bite of lunch around here?" Dix said.

Trixie spent the day cleaning, doing laundry and running errands. She had a nice roast in the oven when Pickford came home.

"Whatever that is, it smells good," he said.

"A roast with potatoes and carrots," Trixie said. "And apple pie for dessert."

"I'll wash up and change and be right with you," Pickford said.

Ten minutes later, Pickford carved the roast and he and Trixie sat down to dinner.

"I heard from Dix today," Pickford said. "He's on his way to Grayson Country."

"He's alright then?" Trixie said.

Pickford smiled. "It's been my experience over the years that when Dix is involved in a case, you should always worry about the other guy."

Chapter Forty-Four

The Grayson County State Prison was home to two-thousand inmates. Dix and Bauer arrived at four in the morning, stayed the night in a small hotel and went to the prison after breakfast.

Warden Ned Harmon saw Dix and Bauer in his office. "Would you mind telling me what a Texas Ranger and federal man are doing in my office?" he said.

"We're here to see a prisoner named Dick Sanders," Dix said.

"What for?" Harmon said.

"You know, warden, you're the second asshole I've met in the last twenty-four hours," Dix said.

"What did . . . you can't speak to me that way," Harmon said. He looked at the prison guard in the corner of his office. "Remove these men," he said.

Dix turned to the guard. "One step closer and you will eat soup for the rest of your natural born days," he said. "Now go find Dick Sanders."

"Warden?" the guard said.

Harmon nodded and the guard left the office.

"You're a hard man, Mr. Federal Officer," Harmon said.

"It's a hard job, Warden," Dix said. "Now suppose you tell me how long this Sanders is going to be your guest."

Harmon stood up, went to a file cabinet and returned with a file, sat and opened it. "Fifteen years," he said.

"Let me see his file," Dix said.

Harmon slid it across his desk and Dix picked it up. "Stagecoach robbery, robbed a general store, stole a wagon and a few other crimes that don't add up to five years," Dix said. "Why fifteen?"

"He and his brother broke out of jail," Harmon said. "His brother got away. He fell off his horse and broke his leg. The ten extra is for jail break."

The guard returned. "Prisoner Sanders is in the hospital, Warden. Recovering from a broken leg," he said.

"Take us to the hospital," Dix said. "Warden, care to join us?"

Harmon stood up. "Why not?" he said. "It's not like I have something else to do around here."

Sanders was in a ward with twenty-three other prisoners.

Dix found the doctor on duty and brought him to Sanders. "Can he be put in a wheelchair?" Dix said.

"Yes, but . . . ?" the doctor said.

"Do it," Dix said. "Warden, is there a room where he can be moved to for a private talk?"

"An examination room?" Harmon said.

"That will do," Dix said.

"What's all this about?" Sanders said.

"If you know what's good for you keep your mouth shut until I ask you a question," Dix said.

Dix rolled a cigarette and gave it to Sanders, then struck a match and lit it for him.

Sitting in a wheelchair, Sanders said, "Thanks, but what's this all about now?"

"This? This is about you going home fifteen years early," Dix said.

"What the hell are you talking about?' Sanders said.

"I'm talking about Bill Longley," Dix said. "What the hell did you think I came here for, to check your broken leg?"

"I had nothing to do with him breaking

us out," Sanders said. "Me and Jim were serving thirty days in the county jail for . . ."

"Public intoxication and breaking up a saloon and sending two deputies to the hospital," Dix said. "A bullshit charge that you turned into 1894 before you see daylight again."

"Like I said, it weren't my idea," Sanders said. "Bill just showed up on his own, got the jump of the deputies and I had the misfortune of falling off the horse he stole cause the saddle wasn't tied proper and here I sit with a busted leg, waiting for, as you said, 1894."

Rolling a cigarette, Dix said, "You're twenty-eight-years-old. Do you know what you're going to look like in fifteen years when you leave this place?"

"Look, law dog, what do you want from me?" Sanders said. "Say it plain."

"Bill Longley, stupid. What did you think?" Dix said. "He had a place in mind he was going when he broke you out. I want to know where that place is."

"You want me to give up my brother Jim?" Sanders said. "He's my flesh."

"He left you in the street with a broken leg, didn't he?" Dix said.

"They was shooting at him," Sanders said.

"Look, stupid, I don't give damn about

your brother," Dix said. "I want Bill Longley and I know that you know where he went."

"I tell you, what I get?" Sanders said.

"You get to go home before you're an old man," Dix said.

"I tell you and I get out of here?" Sanders said.

"What the hell you think we've been talking about?" Dix said.

"I think we talking about I see that in writing first," Sanders said.

"Not concerned about your brother now, are you?" Dix said.

"Screw him," Sanders said. "He left me in the dirt with a broken leg and fifteen years."

"This agreement is contingent upon . . ." Dix said.

"What's that, contingent?" Sanders said.

"That Longley is where you say he is," Dix said. "If he isn't, the deal is off."

"He'll be there," Sanders said.

Dix looked at Harmon. "Warden, do you have a telegraph?"

Dix and Bauer entered the telegraph room at the prison. A guard was at the desk.

"I'm afraid you'll have to leave for a while," Dix said.

"What?" the guard said.

Harmon walked in behind Dix. "It's alright," he said. "Step out for a bit."

The guard left the room. Dix sat at the desk and tapped out a long message to Pickford. "Now we wait," Dix said.

"I'll have some coffee sent in," Harmon said and left the room.

A few minutes later, a guard arrived with a tray that held a coffee pot and two cups. Bauer filled two cups and handed one to Dix.

Dix rolled a cigarette, struck a match and lit it.

"How did you become a Federal Warrant Officer?" Bauer said.

"I was a deputy sheriff in Colorado," Dix said. "While I was delivering a prisoner, a gang of outlaws robbed the bank and my wife was killed. I quit to hunt them down and got a warrant from a judge. He's now a federal judge in Washington and I still work for him as a warrant officer.

"You remarried I see by the ring," Bauer said.

"Not long ago," Dix said.

The key on the telegraph clicked. Dix grabbed a pencil and began to write the response message. When the message was complete, Dix tapped his reply. Then he stood up. "Let's go see Harmon," he said.

■ ■ ■ ■

"Have you pen and ink, Warden?" Dix said.

"You may use my desk," Harmon said.

Harmon stood up, Dix sat down and used pen and ink to write Pickford's message on a sheet of Harmon's letterhead paper.

"Thank you, Warden. Let's go see Sanders," Dix said.

Sanders was back in his bed. Dix handed him the letterhead document. He read it quickly. "Contingent upon the capture of Bill Longley," Sanders said. "Does that mean if you don't get him, I don't get my release?"

"That's what it means, so make it good," Dix said.

"There's this cabin Bill uses to hide out in," Sanders said. "When he broke us out, he said we was going there to hide for a while before robbing a few banks. Like I told you, breaking out of jail weren't my idea, but if you know Bill Longley, it's best to not cross him."

"So where is this hiding place?" Dix said.

"DeSoto Parish in Louisiana," Sanders said. "There's a settlement called Logansport along the Sabine River. There's a thousand places to hide along that river and

Bill has a cabin he uses from time-to-time when he needs to hide. That's where he is. You can take the railroad as far as Shreveport and then you got to ride a good day to reach Logansport. After that, ride along the river. You'll find him. He likes to use the name Bill Jackson."

"And you're sure he's there?" Dix said.

"He's there," Sanders said. "It wouldn't occur to him anybody would ever cross him."

"Hold onto that paper," Dix said. "And if I have to kill your brother, I apologize in advance."

"Go ahead and kill him," Sanders said. "The sum bitch left me in the dirt with a broken leg."

"I'll be in touch and I'm glad to see you're a forgiving brother," Dix said.

"You know where to find me," Sanders said.

"Sergeant Bauer, let's go," Dix said.

Chapter Forty-Five

"Sorry I can't make the trip with you, but I'm not authorized to leave Texas," Bauer said.

"It was good traveling with you," Dix said.

"You too," Bauer said.

They shook hands and Dix boarded the train bound for Shreveport.

A large package from San Francisco was waiting for Trixie at the post office. She took it and the regular mail and hurried home.

She made a pot of coffee in the kitchen and then opened the package from Farber. It contained six sets of blueprints and sketches of ranch homes he designed. Each was meticulously drawn and beautiful. She didn't quite understand all the numbers on the prints, but she got the general idea of the layouts of each home.

After looking at all six homes, she realized she forgot to stop by the market, grabbed her purse and rushed out the door.

At the market, Trixie placed the regular order, then, as she walked home she spotted Angel about to enter the café.

"Angel," Trixie said.

Angel had a stack of mail in her right hand. "I was just looking for you," she said.

"Come back with me. I want to show you something," Trixie said.

"Back where?" Angel said.

"The Judge's house," Trixie said. "It won't take long."

"The Judge has a beautiful home," Angel said as Trixie poured coffee in the kitchen.

"Yes he does," Trixie said. "Now come look at these drawings with me."

They went through the six drawings carefully, checking size, dimensions and styles.

"I like number three the best," Trixie said.

"I'm sort of leaning to it myself," Angel said. "But look at the cost."

The house, barn, bunkhouse, corral and well was listed at eleven-thousand and six hundred dollars.

"None of them are cheap," Trixie said. "That's why Dix is working so hard."

"You have a good man, honey," Angel said. "And I have to get back."

"I'll walk you out," Trixie said.

■ ■ ■ ■

Pickford came home with a telegram from Dix. "He's on the way to Shreveport in Louisiana," he said. "I expect he almost there by now."

"I got the blueprints for the house today," Trixie said. "Will you look at them with me?"

"How long to dinner?" Pickford said.

"Fifteen minutes."

"I'll wash up and change," Pickford said. "We'll look at them after we eat."

Pickford and Trixie studied each blueprint carefully and both agreed on house number three.

"When will Dix be home?" Trixie said.

"Hard to say," Pickford said. "Maybe a week, maybe less, maybe more."

"What do I do?"

"What did Dix ask you to do?" Pickford said.

"He said to use my own judgement," Trixie said. "That he trusted me."

"Then that is what you should do," Pickford said. "Send a telegram to Mr. Farber to begin work on number three."

Trixie nodded.

Pickford grinned.
"It will be fine," Pickford said.

Chapter Forty-Six

Dix got off the train in Shreveport at eight o'clock in the evening. He walked his horse from the depot into the center of town.

It was a nice town of about eight thousand people, most descendants of the old French. Their influence was everywhere, in the streets, buildings, food and language.

Dix found a hotel with a livery, checked in, stabled his horse and had dinner at the hotel restaurant. He ordered a steak that was spicy enough to melt the hair on his head. After that, he went to his room, read the reports on Longley and memorized his face from the lone photograph of the man.

He wanted no mistakes tomorrow. Before turning in, he rolled a cigarette and smoked at the open window and looked at the quiet streets below.

Trixie and Pickford took snifters of brandy

to the backyard table that faced large rose bushes.

"Back in Colorado, every spring, my wife would plant rose bushes," Pickford said. "Even though she was gone by the time I moved to Washington, I have them planted in her memory."

"She must have been quite a lady," Trixie said.

"You remind me of her in certain ways," Pickford said.

"I do?"

"Oh, she didn't have the difficult background that you did, but could be very tough like you when she wanted to be," Pickford said. "She made me tow the line for sure."

Trixie took a sip of brandy. "I dust pictures of you son and daughter, but you never speak of them," Trixie said. "Why is that?"

"Many years ago, my wife told me to never bore people with stories about our children," Pickford said. "She was right, so I don't."

"But I'm interested," Trixie said. "Can you tell me a little something?"

"Well, alright," Pickford said. "My son Jonathan is in the navy for the past fifteen years. He is presently second in command on a ship somewhere in the Chine Seas. My daughter married a New York businessman and lives in Manhattan. I despise Manhattan even more than Washington, but I do my due-diligence and visit Thanksgiving and Christmas."

Trixie sipped some brandy.

"Not the closest of relationships," Pickford said.

"At least you didn't sell them," Trixie said.

Pickford looked at Trixie and laughed.

"This brandy is making me sleepy," Trixie said.

"I, too," Pickford said. "I suggest that we get some sleep."

Chapter Forty-Seven

Dix left Shreveport at dawn and rode north to the Sabine and Logansport, hoping to reach the river by nightfall.

He skipped breakfast to get the early start, so by noon his stomach was rumbling. He stopped, made a fire and put on some breakfast. While bacon and beans cooked in a pan, he fed his horse a sack of grain.

The coffee was ready first and Dix smoked a cigarette as he drank a cup. He had yet to see one person traveling along the road as was often the case in such rural areas.

After eating, Dix rode straight through to nightfall and reached the small settlement of Logansport. It was less than a settlement, really and more of a trading post along the river. There was one large, log cabin surrounded by several tents. A few horses were tied up to a hitching post.

Dix dismounted, tied his horse to the post, stepped up to the porch and entered the cabin. A man behind the counter said, "We're closing, mister."

"I need a few things," Dix said. "I'll be out of here in two minutes."

"What do you need?" the man said.

"Bacon, beans, cornbread, fresh eggs if you have them, salted butter, a sack of coffee, a pouch of tobacco, rolling paper and matches," Dix said.

The clerk got everything together and wrapped it all in brown paper and tied it with string. "That will be ten dollars," he said.

Dix paid the man and carried the sack outside where two men were standing beside his horse.

"You boys want something?" Dix said.

"Nice looking horse," one of the men said.

"He suits me," Dix said.

"Would you sell him?" the second man said.

"Nope," Dix said as he put the sack into his saddlebags.

"Take him in trade?"

"Nope."

"I reckon we just better kill you and take him then," the first man said.

Dix untied the reins. "Horse," he said.

The horse reared up and clubbed the second man on the head with his front hoof.

The man fell unconscious to the ground.

The first man reached for his gun. Dix drew his Colt and clubbed him across the head with it and he joined his friend on the ground.

Dix mounted the saddle. “Let’s go, horse,” he said and rode away.

Once the moon was up, it was easy traveling along the river. Moonlight glistened off the water and occasionally, a fish jumped. Each side of the river was thickly wooded. A cabin could be hid anywhere.

Around ten o’clock, Dix smelled a fire. It was faint, far off.

He dismounted and gave the horse a rest and fed him some grain. He rolled a cigarette and smoked watching the moon glide across the river. A fish jumped and the splash caused moonlit ripples.

After his horse finished his grain, Dix rode for another two hours. He was traveling southeast and with each passing mile, the aroma of smoke grew stronger.

The source wasn’t far off now. Dix stopped his horse and watched the moonlit tree line and sky.

The source of the smoke was maybe a mile off and set back into the woods.

“Let’s go take a look,” Dix said to his horse.

He rode away from the river and into the woods. Three quarters of a mile later, Dix stopped when he heard voices. Two men, laughing drunkenly and jabbering in hushed tones.

Dix dismounted and followed the voices, walking his horse beside him until he was three-hundred-feet from a rundown, shack of a cabin.

A lantern mounted to the wall illuminated two men in chairs. They were pulling on a jug of corn liquor and laughing drunkenly at nothing. Dix used his binoculars to get a closer look at the faces of the two men.

One was Bill Longley. The other had to be Jim Sanders.

Dix watched them empty the jug and Longley tossed it off the porch. "Nuther," he said.

Jim got to his feet and wobbled inside and returned with a fresh jug. He flopped into his chair, pulled the cork and took a swig.

"Don't hog it you sum bitch," Longley said.

Jim passed the jug to Longley.

Dix hid behind a tree to roll and light a cigarette. It wouldn't be long now, he thought. And thirty minutes later, Longley and Jim passed out in a drunken stupor.

Dix mounted up and tugged the reins.

"Let's go, horse," he said.

At the porch of the cabin, Dix dismounted and reached into his saddlebags for two sets of shackles. He went up to the porch where Longley and Jim were passed out cold and shackled their right and left wrists and ankles together.

Dix went into the cabin where the fire was just about out, tossed some wood from the bin into the fireplace and built it back up so in the morning it would be quicker to get it going again. Then he ripped up some rags into strips and tied Longley and Jim to their chairs.

Neither man so much as moved a muscle. Then Dix removed the saddle from his horse. He didn't bother to tie him up. "Eat as much grass as you want, just don't wander off too far," he said.

He removed the bedroll from the saddle, found a comfortable spot in the grass and went to sleep.

Dix opened his eyes when the sun hit him in the face. He stood up, packed up his bedroll and then went up to the porch.

Longley and Jim were still passed out cold in the chairs. Dix entered the cabin, stirred the hot coals and built another fire. Then he returned to his saddlebags for supplies and brought them to the fire.

He put on a pot of coffee, bacon, beans and cooked six fried eggs. When everything was ready, Dix filled a bucket of water from the pump and threw it on Longley and Jim.

They woke with a start, muttered, sputtered, tried to stand but were anchored to the chairs.

"Good morning," Dix said.

Longley and Jim looked at Dix. "Who the hell are you?" Longley said.

'I imagine you must have some headache right about now," Dix said. "Want some food and coffee?"

"You got us chained up like an organ grinder's monkey," Jim said.

"Do you want to eat or not?" Dix said.

"How can we eat hog tied like this?" Longley said. "And who the hell are you anyway?"

"Be right back," Dix said.

He went into the cabin, filled two plates with food and a cup of coffee and returned to the deck. He put a plate on their laps. "Eat with your free hand," Dix said.

Dix went inside and returned with a plate of food and a cup of coffee and sat in a vacant chair.

Eating some bacon, Longley said, "You a bounty hunter, mister?"

Dix tapped the badge on his shirt. "Federal Warrant Officer," he said. "And I have a warrant for your arrest."

"What bout me, you got a warrant for me?" Jim said.

"You broke out of jail, stupid," Dix said. "I don't need a warrant for you."

"You'll never bring me back alive," Longley said.

"Then I'll bring you back dead," Dix said. "At least I won't have to feed you and listen to your stupid talk."

"If there is any justice, you won't live to spend a nickel of that filthy blood money" Longley said.

"Finish your breakfast, we got a long ride ahead of us," Dix said.

"Where we going?" Jim said.

Dix stood up. "Texas, you idiot," he said. "Horse?"

From around the side of the cabin, the horse came running.

"Mr. Farber would like to meet with us in Carson City as soon as possible," Trixie said after she showed the telegram to Pickford .

It was Saturday and Pickford liked a late breakfast on Saturday's. Trixie had time to go to the post office before she prepared the Saturday morning feast.

She made pancakes, bacon, sausage, eggs, coffee and also served orange juice from oranges she squeezed herself.

Pickford read the telegram. “You have to go,” he said.

“I can’t go alone,” Trixie said.

“If Dix isn’t back by Monday, then I shall go with you,” Pickford said.

“I can’t ask you to do that,” Trixie said.

“You didn’t ask,” Pickford said. “Would you pass the bacon please?”

Chapter Forty-Eight

"My ankles hurt," Longley said.

Longley and Jim were in the small holding jail in the last car of the train to Austin. Dix sat in a chair opposite the cell, read a newspaper and smoked a cigarette. He looked up at Longley.

"Thinking of all the innocent people you murdered, I'm not all that moved by your sore ankle," Dix said.

"You're a blood-thirsty murderer is what you are," Longley said. "A butcher."

Dix laughed. "Funny coming from you," he said.

"I ain't killed nobody," Jim said. "This ain't fair by God. All I did was rob a general store and got caught at that."

"You're forgetting the jailbreak," Dix said.

"He did that, not me," Jim said. "Blame him."

"Shut up, Jim, or one day I'll kill you too," Longley said.

"Why is we slowing down?" Jim said.
"We're in Austin, stupid," Dix said.

Dix sat in a chair with a cup of coffee and watched as Captain Foxx wrote a report for him to take back to Washington. Bauer sat beside him.

"Remarkable achievement, Mr. Dix," Bauer said.

"I agree, sergeant," Foxx said. "Mr. Dix, the Rangers could use a man like you."

"Thank you, captain, but I have a wife waiting on me," Dix said. "And then retirement."

Foxx handed Dix the report. "Good luck, sir."

"Thank you, captain," Dix said. "Well, I have a train to catch."

"I'll see you out," Bauer said.

"Why not come to Carson City with us and start over?" Trixie said. "It's never too late, Angel. I mean, look at me. Do you think I would have thought a year ago, I would be married and moving to Nevada?"

Angel sliced off a bit of pie with her fork. "You got lucky," she said. "Dix is an exceptional man."

"He doesn't have to be exceptional," Trixie said. "He just has to love you."

"I'm not sure I know what love is anymore," Angel said.

"You'll know it when you feel it," Trixie said.

"God, I hope you're right," Angel said.

"You'll see," Trixie said. "When the right one comes along, you'll know it."

"Well, I better get back," Angel said.

"Me too," Trixie said. "The judge likes to eat at five on Sunday."

"He's a good man, isn't he the Judge?" Angel said.

"Yes, he is," Trixie said. "A very good man."

"He cares for you a lot, doesn't he?" Angel said.

"He treats me like I was his daughter," Trixie said.

"That's good," Angel said. "Well, I have to get back now. See you soon."

Chapter Forty-Nine

"Remarkable work," Pickford said after he read Dix's report and the report from Captain Foxx in Austin.

"Is Trixie at home?" Dix said.

Pickford looked at the clock on his desk. "She has a regular routine she follows," he said. "The post office, the market and then coffee with her friend Angel. She should be home in about an hour."

"I think I'll go home and take a bath," Dix said.

When Trixie entered the house after her errands, she saw the buckets of hot water on the stove and immediately knew that Dix was home.

She rushed to the bathing room where Dix was in the tub. He grinned at her, "Hello, wife," he said.

Trixie immediately began removing her clothes. "Hello, husband," she said.

"Miss me?" Dix said.

Trixie yanked off her blouse. "A bit," she said. "Why didn't you send a telegram you were coming home?"

"I'd be home before you got it," Dix said.

Trixie, skirt off, yanked at her shoes, stumbled backward and fell on her rear.

"Problem?" Dix said.

Trixie pulled off her shoes and socks, then stood up. "Move over," she said.

She got into the large tub and sat opposite Dix. "Everything went well?" she said.

"It did," Dix said.

Trixie leaned forward and kissed Dix. "I have some news of my own," she said. "Mr. Farber sent us samples to choose from."

"And what did you decide?" Dix said.

"I'll tell you after you look at them," Trixie said as Dix nibbled on her neck and held her close.

"Dix, honey, is that the soap?" Trixie said.

"Nope," Dix said.

As Trixie prepared dinner in the kitchen, Dix studied the samples at the table. He sipped coffee and smoked a cigarette as he carefully reviewed each set of sketches.

"Three," he said. "I like number three."

"So do I," Trixie said. "Did you read Mr. Farber's note about meeting him?"

"I did," Dix said. "What did the Judge say?"

"He said if you weren't back by Monday, he would go with me," Trixie said.

"We'll leave tomorrow," Dix said. "I'll send Farber a telegram in the morning."

"But the Judge . . ."

"I'll ask him if he wants to go with us," Dix said.

"One other thing," Trixie said. "How much did you make this trip?"

"Seventy-five-hundred," Dix said. "After paying Farber, we'll still have about twenty-five-thousand left. In a year . . ."

"Between what I had saved up and working for the Judge, I have two-thousand-dollars," Trixie said. "I'd like to add that to the . . ."

"Keep saving that," Dix said. "In an emergency, we may need it."

"Okay, clear and set the table," Trixie said. "The judge will be home any minute."

"Yes ma'am," Dix said.

"We'll leave tomorrow morning after you deposit the latest reward money," Pickford said.

"Are you sure?" Dix said.

"I've been thinking about what you said about how Carson City might need a judge, or even a lawyer," Pickford said. "I am a lawyer, you know."

"I guess we better pack," Trixie said.

"Can we have the pie you made for dessert first?" Dix said.

Except for some moonlight shining through the window, the room was dark and quiet.

Trixie stirred and reached over and gently shook Dix awake. "Dix, honey?" she said.

Dix opened his eyes. "What is it?" he said.

"I'm afraid that something might go wrong," Trixie said.

"With what?"

"Anything. Everything. I don't know."

Dix rolled over and Trixie placed her head on his chest. "We got the expense of the house covered with twenty-five-thousand left over," he said. "Six more months maybe and I can quit and we'll go west and start our ranch."

"Is that all you want to start?" Trixie said.

"Now that you mention it," Dix said.

Chapter Fifty

Dix played chess with Pickford in Pickford's sleeper car. "It's your move, Judge," Dix said.

"Don't rush me," Pickford said. "Chess is a game not to be rushed."

Trixie entered the car with a coffee pot and went to the table. "You're going to miss supper," she said as she filled two cups beside the chessboard.

"Did you reserve our table?" Pickford said.

"For seven o'clock," Trixie said.

Dix looked at his pocket watch. "You got thirty minutes to make a move," he said.

"Don't rush me," Pickford said.

"Is this the same move from before I went to get coffee?" Trixie said.

"The Judge doesn't like to be rushed," Dix said.

"You be quiet," Pickford said.

"I'm going to change," Trixie said. "I'll be

back in ten minutes."

After Trixie left, Pickford made his move and placed Dix in check. "And that, I believe, is checkmate," he said.

Dix studied the board.

"Well?" Pickford said.

"Don't rush me," Dix said.

Trixie returned, wearing a fresh blouse and with her hair up. "Dinner, boys. Finish this later," she said.

"Come on, Judge," Dix said.

"Saved by the bell," Pickford said.

They left the sleeper car and walked along the hallway to the next car and then the next, which was a riding car. As they walked through the car, a man suddenly slapped the woman who was with him.

"You'll do what I tell you," the man said.

"All I said was . . ." the woman said and the man slapped her again.

The woman fell out of her seat.

"I'll learn you," the man said and was about to slap the woman again when Dix grabbed his hand and yanked him out of his seat.

"That's enough," Dix said.

"Who in blazes are you?" the man said.

"I don't like men who hit women?" Dix said.

"I don't give a goddamn what you don't

like," the man said.

Dix slapped the man four, five, six times and the man fell into his seat.

"Miss, are you alright?" Dix said to the woman.

She looked up at Dix. Her cheek was red from the slaps. She looked at the man. "That's the last time you hit me," she said.

The man started to get up and Dix shoved him back down. "Miss, come with us," Dix said.

"You can't . . ." the man said and Dix knocked him unconscious with a solid punch to the jaw.

The woman stood and Trixie took her arm. "Are you hurt?" Trixie said.

"Not nearly as much as when he gets me later," she said.

"He won't," Pickford said

A conductor entered the car. "What's happening here?" he said.

Pickford said, "That man was beating this woman. My associate put a stop to it."

The conductor looked at the woman. "Are you hurt, miss?"

"I'll be alright," she said.

"I'm federal judge Alan Pickford from Washington. My associate here is Federal Warrant Officer Dix," Pickford said. "I suggest he lock this man up in your prisoner car for the duration of your schedule for this woman's protection."

The conductor nodded. "Get him up and follow me," he said.

"Dix, join us in the dining car," Pickford said.

"Are you really a judge?"

"Yes, I'm really a judge?" Pickford said. "Now, who are you?"

"My name is Katherine Russell, but everybody calls me Kate."

"What was that all about back there?" Pickford said.

"That man is my brother," Kate said.

"Your brother?" Trixie said.

"I'm sorry to say, but yes, my brother," Kate said. "We are traveling to San Francisco to attend the reading of our father's will. My brother is a gambler and a drunkard. He wants me to give him my share and I refused."

"Miss Russell, I will see to it that your brother won't interfere with your father's last wishes," Pickford said.

"Can you do that?" Kate said.

"He sure can," Dix said as he arrived at the table and sat beside Trixie.

"My husband, Dix," Trixie said.

"I wish to thank you for helping me, Mr.

Dix," Kate said.

"No need. Are you hurt?" Dix said.

"He's done worse," Kate said.

"That man is her brother," Trixie said.

"Your brother?" Dix said.

The waiter came to the table.

"Let's order," Pickford said. "We can talk about all this later."

Dix, already in bed, watched Trixie brush her hair.

"You didn't hesitate one second to help her," Trixie said. "You are an admirable man, my husband."

"I don't like men who hit women," Dix said.

"Do you think the judge can really help her?"

"Don't bet against him," Dix said.

Trixie put the brush down and got into bed. "Who won the chess game?" she said.

"I'd rather not talk about it," Dix said.

"Don't be a sore loser," Trixie said.

Dix lowered the lamp beside the bed and the room fell dark.

"And don't pout," Trixie said as she rolled on top of him.

Chapter Fifty-One

Dix and Trixie got off in Carson City. Judge Pickford continued on to San Francisco with Kate. Farber was already at the Carson City Hotel and met Dix and Trixie in the lobby.

It was late afternoon, too late in the day to ride out to the property, but Dix, Trixie and Farber made plans to review his latest sketches before dinner.

After checking in and dropping their luggage in their room, Dix and Trixie met Farber in the hotel library.

"I made additional sketches of house number three, along with the bunkhouse and barn, using colored pencils," Farber said. "The color brings out the details of the wood and paint."

Dix and Trixie studied the sketches. They were beautiful done and the color highlighted certain features that were lost in the black and white sketches.

"I've taken care of the materials needed locally, but the work crew is the crew I've used for years and will be from San Francisco," Farber said. "They will live on site in tents until the job is complete. The first order of business is to locate the well and lay pipes to the house and bunkhouse. Two of the work crew will ride with us to the site in the morning and begin the process."

"I wired funds to the bank in Carson City before we left Washington," Dix said. "We'll take care of that first before we ride to the site."

"Excellent," Farber said. "And now, as I am starving, I suggest dinner."

"Mr. and Mrs. Dix, this is Thomas Mitchel," Farber said. "He's part of the crew and has been planning wells for me for fifteen years."

Mitchel shook hands with Dix and Trixie. "Nice to know you," he said. "Now, having surveyed this land for the past two days with Mr. Farber, my recommendation is to dig the well thirty feet from the house and pipe it to the kitchen and bunkhouse. If there is ever a problem with the well, we don't have to tear up the house to get to it."

Farber said, "Let's walk and mark the dimensions with stakes."

Three hours later, the house, barn, bunkhouse and corral were staked and outlined with rough twine.

"We'll begin work tomorrow," Farber said. "Would you like to be on hand to watch the first dig?"

"We would," Dix said.

Dix, Trixie and Farber had dinner in the hotel dining room.

"How long will you be staying in Carson City?" Farber asked.

"Until the Judge returns from San Francisco," Dix said.

"Which he has," Trixie said.

Walking to the table, Pickford smiled at Trixie. "Mr. Farber, how are you," he said.

"Just fine, Judge," Farber said. "You're just in time. We haven't ordered yet."

Pickford sat beside Trixie.

"How did it go with Kate?" she said.

"I met with the deciding judge and he agreed the assets from the will be shared equally," Pickford said. "I also took steps to ensure that Kate's brother have no further contact with her for her protection."

"Where is she now?" Dix said.

"Changing her blouse," Pickford said.

"She came back with you?" Dix said.

"She doesn't want to return to Boston,"

Pickford said. "Where she teaches school. She'd like to . . . well, I let her tell you that herself."

Kate approached the table. "Hello, everyone," she said.

"Kate, this is Mr. Farber, the architect I told you about," Pickford said.

Farber stood and shook Kate's hand. "Delighted," he said.

"Thank you," Kate said.

Pickford stood and held the chair next to him for Kate to sit. "Thank you, Judge," she said.

"I was about to tell them your plans, but I'll leave that up to you now," Pickford said.

"It's simple, really," Kate said. "In Boston, I am one in ten-thousand teachers. Out here, I am much more needed than back east. I'd like to settle where I am needed most."

"That's a fine idea," Trixie said. "Would you like to take a ride with us in the morning to our . . . Dix, what do we call it?"

"Home," Dix said.

"We'll see you out there," Pickford said. He, Farber and Kate were in a rented buggy at the local livery stables.

"We'll be right behind you," Dix said.

Trixie looked at the bay Dix rented for

her. "She looks awful big, Dix," she said.

"She's the smallest they have, hon," Dix said. "And gentle."

"I haven't worn britches since I can't remember when," Trixie said.

"They look kind of good on you," Dix said. "Now, are you ready."

"What do I do?" Trixie said.

"See that horn on the saddle? Grab that, put your left foot in the stirrup and lift yourself into the saddle," Dix said.

Trixie grabbed the horn, put her left boot in the stirrup and sort of danced around while the horse walked in circle.

"This isn't working," Trixie said.

"Hold on," Dix said, grabbed Trixie by the rear and lifted her up and into the saddle.

Did anybody see that?" Trixie said.

"Just the horse," Dix said. He mounted his horse and said, "Let's go."

"Go? How do you make it start?" Trixie said.

"Give the reins a gentle yank and your horse will follow mine," Dix said.

Dix yanked his reins and moved his horse out of the livery and Trixie's horse followed.

"Stay behind me until we're out of town, then pull up next to me," Dix said.

"Are you talking to me or the horse?"

Trixie said.

After they left town, Dix had Trixie move up beside him and they rode a solid five miles before Trixie needed to take a break.

"My legs and back," Trixie said.

"Your bounce is off," Dix said.

"My what?"

"Bounce," Dix said. "Try to bounce with the horse and not against it. That will save a lot of backaches."

After s short rest, the mounted up and Trixie did her best to bounce with the motion of her horse rather that against it.

"Better?" Dix said.

"Yes."

Trixie made the rest of the ride without stopping until they reached the site where Pickford, Farber, Mitchel and Kate waited for them.

Dix helped Trixie dismount and they joined the group.

"Mr. Dix, it's traditional to let the man in charge dig the first shovel," Mitchel said.

"In this case," Dix said. "The man in charge is her," he said and handed the shovel to Trixie.

Grinning, Trixie dug the first shovelful of dirt.

Chapter Fifty-Two

"She's a nice woman. I hope it works out for her," Trixie said.

"She inherited twenty-five-thousand dollars," Pickford said. "She will be just fine."

"What about you?" Dix said.

"A position as judge is available to me if I want it," Pickford said.

"Do you?" Trixie said. "Want it?"

"Small court, much shorter hours, I believe I do," Pickford said. "It's a nice way to spend my old age."

"And you'll live with us?" Trixie said.

"If you don't mind a cantankerous old man under foot, I believe I will," Pickford said. "But you must allow me to contribute. I'm not a poor man, you know. Far from it."

"On weekends you can work as a hand to pay for your keep," Dix said.

The waiter came by their table in the dining car on the train.

"We missed breakfast, so bring us everything," Pickford said.

In Pickford's sleeper car, Dix and Pickford played a game of chess. Pickford played white, Dix the black.

After twenty moves, the game was equal. Both men had small glasses of whiskey they barely touched. After Pickford took a pawn from Dix, Dix rolled a cigarette as he studied the board.

As he lit the cigarette, Dix said, "I have twenty-five-thousand left. I'll need forty to make this work, Judge. I won't shortchange Trixie."

"My boy, Trixie would live in a ten as long as it's with you," Pickford said. "Don't you know that?"

"Maybe so, but I won't shortchange her on this," Dix said. "Not after the life she's had. I'll work until I have forty. You'll see to that."

"I'll see to it if you ever decide to make your next move," Pickford said.

"Don't rush me," Dix said.

Trixie was brushing her hair at the small dresser in their sleeper car when Dix entered and immediately started to undress.

"Who won the game?" she said.

"I'd rather not talk about it," Dix said as he sat on the bed and removed his boots.

Trixie looked away to hide her grin.

"We'll be home in the morning," Dix said. "I need to get back to work if we're to buy enough cattle to make this ranch successful."

"Dix, you heard what the Judge said," Trixie said. "He said he'd contribute his own money to . . ."

"Trixie, sometimes a man has to finish what he starts," Dix said. "I hope you can understand that."

Trixie set the brush aside and stood up. "I understand," she said. "And I admire you for it. All I ask is you don't get killed before we have the chance to start the ranch."

Dix got into bed. "I'm not so . . ."

"Easy to kill," Trixie said. "Yes, I know. Move over."

Chapter Fifty-Three

Pickford was in his chambers, catching up on paperwork when a court officer knocked on the door. "Judge?" the officer said.

"Enter," Pickford said.

The officer entered the chambers. "A man here to see you, Judge. He says he's an old friend," he said.

"What's his name?" Pickford said.

"James Cohan, Judge."

Pickford was stunned for a moment. Then he said, "Send him in."

The officer nodded and closed the door.

Pickford stood up and walked to the door. It opened and Cohan entered. "Alan," Cohan said.

"Jimmy," Pickford said.

They shook hands and embraced.

"You old lawyer, what are you doing here?" Pickford said.

"I came to ask for your help," Cohan said.

"Before you ask anything, how have you

been?" Pickford said.

"I've temporarily closed my practice, Alan," Cohan said.

"Why?"

"Alan, would you have anything to drink?" Cohan said.

"Have a seat," Pickford said. He went to the small bar in the corner of the office and poured two small drinks of whiskey. He gave one to Cohan and took his chair behind his desk.

"Now, what's on your mind, Jimmy?" Pickford said.

"My youngest son was murdered," Cohan said.

"Andy?" Pickford said. "How? Why?"

Cohan took a sip of his drink. "You know the ranch I bought in Arizona near Tucson?"

"Twenty-years ago, wasn't it?" Pickford said.

"Three of my four sons work and live on the ranch," Cohan said. "My oldest is a lawyer and part of my firm."

"So what happened for God's sake?" Pickford said.

"Six months ago, Andy got into some kind of altercation with a homesteader named Valdez," Cohan said. "This Valdez beat Andy to death with his bare hands."

"My God," Pickford said.

"When his brothers found him dead in the barn, they said Andy's face was pulp," Cohan said.

"How do you know it was this Valdez?" Pickford said.

"They were seen arguing in town the day before," Cohan said. "When my two sons rode over to his homestead, he had packed up and left. Took his wife and son and disappeared."

"Jim, I'm sorry about all of this, but you haven't told me how I can help you," Pickford said.

"I hired a private detective agency to locate Valdez," Cohan said. "He's somewhere along the Pecos River in Texas near the Rio Grande, but they don't know exactly where. I understand you have a man working for you that's supposed to be the best. I want you to swear out a warrant for the arrest of Valdez and I'm offering a twenty-five-thousand-dollar reward."

"I assume you're talking about Dix," Pickford said. "He isn't a bounty hunter, he's a dully sworn federal warrant officer."

"Then swear out a federal warrant and I'll offer the reward," Cohan said.

"Jim, I can't make it dead or alive," Pickford said. "You have no witnesses, evidence or proof. I can swear out a warrant for his arrest and he'll stand trial. That's the best I can do."

"That's good enough, Alan," Cohan said. "I'll take my chances in court."

"Do you have any documentation I can use?" Pickford said.

"A report from the sheriff concerning the argument in town between Andy and Valdez," Cohan said. "Valdez struck Andy before a deputy broke it up. My other two sons documented that when they rode to Valdez's homestead, they had vacated the premises."

"Is that it?" Pickford said.

"I know it's circumstantial, but It's enough to bring him in for questioning," Cohan said.

"I agree," Pickford said. "Now, where are you staying?"

"Nowhere yet. I just got here," Cohan said.

"Then you'll stay with me tonight," Pickford said. "You'll get to meet Dix. His wife is my housekeeper."

"How did that happen?" Cohan said.

"Long story," Pickford said. "We'll talk about it tonight."

Dix, Pickford and Cohan had a glass of whiskey after dinner in Pickford's study.

"Mr. Dix, your wife is one hell of a cook," Cohan said. "That was the best meal I've had since my misses passed away."

"Appreciate that, Mr. Cohan," Dix said. "Now about this Valdez. The Judge filled me in earlier. How sure are you he's down along the Pecos?"

"I'll give you the reports from the private detective," Cohan said. "He has family and friends down there protecting him. To finish this job requires a man like yourself. Fearless, an expert at bringing men in to justice."

"I told Jim I can issue a dead or alive warrant," Pickford said. "Valdez has to stand trial. That's the way it has to be."

"Understood," Dix said. "Mr. Cohan, I'd like all documents to study, including any sketches of Valdez."

"Not a problem," Cohan said.

"I'll leave day after tomorrow," Dix said.

"Excellent," Cohan said. "And now I'd like to get some sleep. I am very tired from the trip."

"Goodnight, Jim," Pickford said.

After Cohan left the study, Pickford said, "What do you think?"

"It's certainly enough to bring him in for questioning," Dix said. "And I'm no lawyer, but I don't see how he's convicted on such flimsy evidence."

"I agree, but Jim is one of my oldest friends," Pickford said. "We went to law school together. He's one of the finest defense attorney's in the country. He knows all the angles and tricks a defense attorney can use in court, so he'll be prepared for Valdez to fight and possibly win."

"That isn't what concerns me," Dix said. "A cougar will run until its cornered, then it will fight. Valdez isn't going without a fight, Judge. I don't want to kill a man who may not be guilty."

"Find a way to bring him in alive," Pickford said.

"If I even find him," Dix said.

Chapter Fifty-Four

"How long will you be gone?" Trixie

"I don't know," Dix said. said. "A few weeks at least."

"Twenty-five-thousand?" Trixie said.

"That's what Mr. Cohan is offering," Dix said. "So this should be my last job. We'll have enough to start our ranch."

"Don't do anything stupid like get killed," Trixie said. "I need you, don't you know that?"

"Last job and we head west," Dix said.

"When are you going?"

"Day after tomorrow."

Trixie picked up her brush and started brushing her hair. "This doesn't feel right to me," she said.

"Going after an outlaw never feels right," Dix said. "But it has to be done."

"I'm not talking about that," Trixie said. "Oh, I don't know what I'm talking about. Just come back to me is all I ask."

"You don't have to ask," Dix said. "I'll never leave you."

Trixie dropped the brush and rushed to Dix, who was removing his boots. "You ever do and I'll hunt you down and give you a teste of your own medicine," she said.

"Let's get some sleep," Dix said.

"I have a better idea," Trixie said.

After breakfast, while Pickford went to court, Cohan and Dix took a walk around Washington.

"A great deal has changed since I last walked around Washington," Cohan said. "Grant was being inaugurated and the population was fifty-thousand less."

They walked to the park near The White House and found a bench near in the shade of cherry trees.

Dix rolled a cigarette and Cohan lit a cigar.

"You've known the Judge a long time?" Cohan said.

"Seven or eight years," Dix said.

"He's the best man I know," Cohan said.

"Can't disagree with you on that," Dix said.

"You won't kill this man," Cohan said. "I want him to stand trial for what he's done. To know what the word justice means."

"Mr. Cohan, outlaws don't always cooperate," Dix said. "If my life is threatened, I might have to kill him. I will do everything I can to bring him back alive, short of allowing him to kill me."

"Understood," Cohan said. "Either way, the money is yours."

"Mr. Cohan, is there anything I should know about your boy?" Dix said. "Was he ever in trouble before? Anything you can tell me about him."

"He was eighteen-years-old," Cohan said. "Do you remember being eighteen?"

"Vividly," Dix said. "I was head of a sniper squad for Sherman."

Cohan nodded. "Alan said you were an extraordinary man, Mr. Dix. I have faith you will bring Valdez in alive."

"About your son?"

"He was a good boy," Cohan said. "Oh, no saint by any means, but he did his work, did well in school and was well liked in the community."

"How much time did you spend at the ranch?" Dix said.

"Not much, but his older brothers made him tow the line," Cohan said. "I would have been aware of any trouble."

"This man Valdez, was he in any trouble prior to this?" Dix said.

"Not that I'm aware of," Cohan said. "But who really knows? There is nothing about prior incidents between him and my son in the sheriff's reports and neither of my other two sons are aware of any."

"I suppose it doesn't really matter in the long run," Dix said. "He'll have his day in court and it will all come out."

"Shall we walk some more?" Cohan said.

They walked around the park and exited near The Halls of Congress.

"A man should never outlive his wife and child," Cohan said. "The feeling inside is pure despair. That's the only way I can describe it. Despair."

"I know the feeling," Dix said.

"You?"

"My first wife was murdered," dix said. "She was pregnant at the time."

"My God," Cohan said.

"It was long before I met Trixie," Dix said.

"Shall we head back? Cohan said. "I'd like to take a nap before dinner."

"How did it go?" Angel said.

"Wonderful," Trixie said. "Work has started on the house. It should be done in four months or so."

They were in the café, having coffee and pie. Trixie had an armload of mail after placing her order at the market.

"Where is Dix now?" Angel said.

"Home until tomorrow," Trixie said. "An old friend of the Judge offered a twenty-five-thousand-dollar reward for finding the man who murdered his son. After that, we head west. And I want to talk to you about that. Come with us."

"Where? Nevada?" Angel said.

"Why not? Nobody out there knows about the saloon," Trixie said. "Start over. Carson City is a nice town with good people. You'd fit right in and we'll be close by and help you get started."

"But what would I do?" Angel said. "The only way I know how to make a living is . . . well, on my back."

"Don't say that to me," Trixie said. "Don't ever say that to me again. You're a beautiful, and smart woman. You could be anything you want. Do you think a year ago I would be married and working for a judge and moving to Nevada? Don't sell yourself short. You have a lot to offer. Remember that."

"Nevada, huh?" Angel said.

"And why not?" Trixie said.

"Well, I'll think about it," Angel said.

"Four months," Trixie said. "Once we go, we're not coming back. So don't take too long thinking."

Angel grinned. "Okay, I won't take too long," she said.

Dix read all the documents a second time at the kitchen table as he drank a cup of coffee. There was a photograph of Valdez, his wife and son that was taken four years according to the date on the back of the tintype.

Valdez, first name Robert, was slightly taller than average height. He was Mexican, with dark hair and eyes and a look about him that spoke of hardship. His wife Maria, also Mexican, was what the city boys called a stargazer. Beautiful face, dark hair and eyes and a fine figure. Their son Peter was around four-years-old in the photograph.

What could their argument have been about that so enraged Valdez that he beat an eighteen-year-old boy to death?

"Dix, are you in the kitchen?" Trixie said from the living room.

"At the table," Dix said.

Trixie entered the kitchen with an armload of mail and set it on the counter. "Everything alright, hon?" she said.

Dix nodded. "I'm going to take a shave and a bath, then pack for tomorrow," he said.

"I'll get some water boiling and then start dinner, so don't take too long," Trixie said.

Dix gathered up all the documents and said, "I won't."

Trixie prepared a tender pot roast with roasted potatoes and carrots, freshly baked rolls, a small salad and blueberry pie and coffee for dessert.

After dinner, Cohan went for a walk. Dix and Pickford went to Pickford's study.

"Pour us a whiskey, would you?" Pickford said.

Dix went to the bar and poured two glasses of bourbon and gave one to Pickford.

"Judge, something isn't adding up about this," Dix said. "Just a feeling I have."

"I'm having the same feeling," Pickford said.

"A man just doesn't beat a boy to death without something triggering it," Dix said. "Maybe a dispute over land or water rights? I think I'll head to Tucson and ask some questions before going to Texas."

"That's a good idea," Pickford said.

"Don't mention it to Mr. Cohan," Dix said. "I'd rather he not know."

"Agreed."

"I'm not sure how long I'll be gone," Dix

said. "Could you and Trixie check on the progress on the house?"

"We'll take a trip in two weeks," Pickford said. "By then you should be down along the Pecos River."

"Appreciate it, Judge," Dix said.

"Now, why don't you go spend the rest of the night with your wife," Pickford said.

Chapter Fifty-Five

Trixie hugged Dix tightly around the waist. She felt the urge to cry, but fought it back and instead forced a tiny smile.

"The next train ride will be to Carson City on a one-way ticket," Dix said.

"You bet," Trixie said.

The conductor called all aboard and Dix said, "Got to go now, hon. I'll wire you from Tucson."

Trixie nodded. She watched Dix board the train and waited until it left the platform and was out of sight. Only then did she turn and walk home.

Pickford drove Cohan to the station later in the afternoon for the four o'clock, east-bound train to New York City.

"Thank you for everything, Alan," Cohan said when they arrived at the station.

"I'll keep you posted every step of the way," Pickford said.

Cohan stepped down from the buggy, grabbed his suitcase and nodded to Pickford. "Take care, Jimmy," Pickford said.

Dix purchased a sleeping car ticket for the two-day ride to Tucson. He spent the morning in his car with a pot of coffee and a novel titled Black Beauty.

It was written by Anna Sewell, who died just five months after its publication. It was an odd novel in the fact that it was written in the first person and the horse Black Beauty was the narrator.

Dix read fifty pages before lunch and another ten while he ate in the dining car. After lunch came a one hour stop and Dix took some carrots to his horse in the boxcar. As the horse munched on carrots, Dix gave him a good brushing until the conductor called all aboard.

Back in his sleeper car, Dix studied the reports once again. The Tucson's doctor's report stated that Andrew Cohan, age eighteen, was beaten to death without the use of a weapon. The autopsy report listed cause of death as brain seepage. He was hit so many times his brain dislodged and floated around inside his skull. It took thirty-six to forty-eight hours for him to die. He never regained consciousness.

Valdez was in an uncontrollable rage. Afterward, when he calmed down and realized what he had done, he packed up and ran.

Reports said Valdez was born in Texas and had family and friends along the Pecos River. They were probably hiding him and his family.

Valdez probably heard every derogatory word and term for Mexicans, so it probably wasn't something that Andy called him that set him off. Maybe Andy called his wife something?

Dix though about what he would if someone called Trixie a name. He'd put that man in his place, but he wouldn't beat him to death.

Dix looked at the photograph of Valdez. He didn't have the look of a killer in his eyes the was Longley or many others did. He had the look of a farmer struggling to make ends meet and put food on the table.

He put the reports away and went to the dining car for a cup of coffee. He rolled and lit a cigarette and thought some more about Valdez.

He was a farmer according to the reports, squatting on twenty-five acres of land signed over to him by the county. Twenty-five acres might get him enough food to see him and his family through the winter, but what did he do for money?

How did he put clothes on his wife and son?

Maybe he'd get some answers in Tucson?

Trixie fixed the Judge one of his favorite evening meals, Irish Stew made with lamb, potatoes and carrots, with warm soda bread lathered with butter.

"My mother used to make this for me every Sunday dinner," Pickford said.

"I learned how to cook from the madam on the wagon," Trixie said. "She was Irish and until I was old enough, my job was to cook. Please don't tell Dix I told you that."

"I won't, but don't you think you can tell him anything?" Pickford said.

"I know, but I don't feel the need to remind him of where I come from," Trixie said. "God knows I try hard to forget."

"Let me tell you something," Pickford said. "You look down to nobody. Hold your head up high. If you were my daughter, I would be very proud of you. Hell, you're not my daughter and I'm still very proud of you."

Trixie teared up and bit and nodded. "Thank you, Judge," she said.

"Is there any more of that soda bread?"

Pickford said.

After dinner, Dix returned to his sleeper car and picked up the copy of Black Beauty and read until he fell asleep with the book on his chest.

Chapter Fifty-Six

"I've thought about what you said," Angel said. "If, in four months you still want me to go to Nevada with you, I'll go."

Trixie reached across the table to squeeze Angel's hand. "You won't regret it, I promise," Trixie said.

"I have some money saved," Angel said. "About twelve-hundred-dollars. Enough to get off to a good start."

"Don't worry about that at all," Trixie said. "In fact, why don't you quit the saloon and come stay with us?"

"I can't quit just yet," Angel said. "Not without Marty getting suspicious. He lost you and hasn't gotten over it yet."

"Marty can go to hell," Trixie said.

"I promise I'll quit when the time is right," Angel said.

"Make it soon," Trixie said.

Tucson was a town of about seven-thousand-residents and built in the Sonoran Desert and surrounded by mountains. As he walked his horse from the depot into town, Dix was struck by the dry heat that was in the mid-nineties, exceptionally hot for September.

Tucson was an eclectic mix of rancher and farmer, white and Mexican and a fairly successful, western town.

Dix's first stop was the sheriff's office, located on Main Street. Dix tied his horse to the post and entered the sheriff's office, where Sheriff Tom Highmore was behind his desk.

A twenty-year veteran in law enforcement, Highmore worked dozens of town as a deputy before being elected sheriff of Tucson.

Highmore looked at the badge pinned to Dix's shirt. "Can I help you?" he said.

Dix removed the warrant from his shirt pocket and set it on the desk. "From Federal Judge Pickford in Washington," Dix said.

Highmore picked up the warrant and read it. "Are you Dix?" he said.

"I am," Dix said.

"Had lunch yet?"

"Just got off the train."

"Come on," Highmore said.

Across the street was a cantina where they

ordered a lunch of rice, beans, fried eggs, bread and coffee.

"How much do you know about this?" Highmore said.

"Just what I read in the reports," Dix said.

"Look, nobody knows what the argument was about between Andy and Valdez," Highmore said. "My deputies broke it up and neither man would say a word about it. Andy rode home and so did Valdez. The next day, Andy was found beaten to death in the barn on the Cohan ranch by his brothers."

"And then?" Dix said

"They suspected Valdez, rode out to his homestead and found the place deserted. Now nobody saw what happened, but why would Valdez run if he wasn't guilty?"

"That's a hard question to answer," Dix said.

"Let me ask you this," Highmore said. "If you know Valdez is somewhere down in the Pecos, what are you doing here?"

"Just being thorough," Dix said. "Trial lawyers, especially defense attorneys have a way of twisting facts to suit their needs."

"I've sat in on a few trials in my time, Mr. Dix. I've seen them twist things around so you wonder who did what to whom," Highmore said.

"And that's why I'm here," Dix said. "So tell me about Andy?"

"He was eighteen," Highmore said. "Do you remember being eighteen? He would rather be in town with the ladies than working the ranch, but you could say that about anybody his age."

"Was he ever in trouble?"

"If you mean with the law, the answer is no," Highmore said. "If you mean with his brothers, that's another story."

"What about Valdez?"

"Bob worked his twenty-five acres. Grew vegetables and melons, mostly for himself and family," Highmore said. "What he did to make money was break horses. Around here, nobody did it better than Bob. He broke horses for the army and just about every ranch within fifty miles, including the Cohan Ranch. I have no proof of it, but I speculated that's what the argument was about. Valdez contracted to break a dozen horses for the Cohan's."

"What do the brothers say?" Dix said.

"Valdez contracted to break a dozen horses for them at ten dollars a horse," Highmore said. "He broke them, but the altercation happened before they could pay him."

"And nobody in town heard what the

argument was about?" Dix said.

"Nobody I could find," Highmore said.

"Can you tell me where the Cohan Ranch is located?" Dix said.

"I'll run you out there after lunch," Highmore said. "Got a hotel room?"

"Not yet."

"The Vista is the biggest right there across the street," Highmore said. "If you like quiet I suggest the Tucson."

"I'll go with quiet," Dix said.

The Cohan Ranch was located ten miles west of Tucson. It was a fifteen-thousand-acre ranch that generally ran two thousand plus head of cattle. The oldest brother, James Jr. was thirty-one. Next was Michael at twenty-nine. Andy, at eighteen had been the youngest and a surprise birth.

James and Michael were at the corral with a few hands, working with some horses.

"Sheriff," James and when Highmore and Dix arrived.

"James, Michael, a word with you," Highmore said.

"Let's go up to the porch," James said.

Seated on the porch, Hightower said, "Boys, this is Federal Warrant Officer Dix. He will be tracking Valdez."

"Then what the hell are you doing here?"

Michael said. "Valdez is down around the Pecos."

"Michael, is it? Take a different tone," Dix said. "Better yet, shut up."

"Calm down, Mike," James said. "Mr. Dix, how can we help you?"

"Have you ever been in a court room when two lawyers are battling it out?" Dix said.

"When we were kids, we'd sometimes watch our father in court," James said.

"You've seen what a lawyer can do with facts," Dix said. "Twist the truth so the innocent man seems guilty and the guilty man goes free. In this case there are no witnesses and no one knows what the argument was about, so if you want Valdez to be punished, I need some facts to go on."

"You don't think it's a bit coincidental Valdez left town right after our brother was murdered?" Michael said.

"And that's what a defense lawyer will say in court, that's it's just a coincidence," Dix said. "Prove it wasn't if you can."

"He's right, Michael," James said. "We can't."

Michael nodded. "I guess so," he said.

"Valdez break horses for you?" Dix said.

"Over the years, sixty or seventy," James said.

"He's good?" Dix said.

"No question he knows what he's doing," James said.

"And he left without being paid for the last twelve," Michael said. "Wouldn't that be considered suspicious?"

"His lawyer will tell you he told you to mail it to him," Dix said. "His word against yours."

"Are you saying the man who beat our brother to death is going to get off?" Michael said.

"I'm not saying anything," Dix said. "My job is to bring him in, not judge him. That's up to a jury."

"Well, you must know what you're doing if you work for the federal courts," James said. "Did my Pa swear out the warrant?"

"He did," Dix said. "In Judge Pickford's court in Washington DC."

"So that's where that old hay shaker wound up," Michael said.

"You see Mr. Pickford, you tell him we said hello," James said.

"I'll do that," Dix said.

"Boys," Highmore said.

Dix sent a telegram home before taking a shave and a bath at the Tucson Inn. The inn was located two blocks off Main Street on a tree-lined, side street. It catered to businessmen wanting a quiet place to stay while in town.

They had their own livery out back and restaurant off the lobby. Dix took advantage of both. He was having coffee and pie after a steak when Sheriff Highmore entered the restaurant with a tall, older man by his side.

"Mr. Dix, we need a moment of your time," Highmore said.

"Have a seat. Order a coffee on me," Dix said.

Highmore and the man took chairs opposite Dix.

"Mr. Dix, this is Louis," Highmore said. "Louis is the town . . . character."

"He means drunk," Louie said.

"Now Louie," Highmore said.

The waitress came to the table. "Coffee for the sheriff and Louie," Dix said.

"I'd rather have a whiskey," Louie said.

"Bring Louie a whiskey," Dix said.

The waitress nodded and left the table.

"Now Louie, tell Mr. Dix what you told me earlier," Highmore said.

"Mr. Timmons lets me sleep in the stables in exchange for cleaning them every day," Louie said. "He also pays me fifty cents a day."

The waitress returned with coffee for

Highmore and a shot of whiskey for Louie. "I thank you kindly," Louie said.

"Go on, Louie," Dix said.

"Sometimes Mr. Jonas at the freight office lets me run freight if he's short a driver," Louie said. "Somebody was sick and he asked me to take a wagon to Casa Grande for ten dollars. So, I did. On the way back, I passed Mr. Valdez in his wagon. It looked like he had everything he owned in there. The odd thing was that his wife was driving the wagon because his hands were wrapped in bandages."

"Bandages? You're sure?" Dix said.

"I'm sure," Louie said.

"You didn't touch your drink," Dix said.

Louie picked up the shot glass and tossed back the whiskey in one easy motion.

"Sheriff, where does that road go?" Dix said.

"Straight run to Phoenix," Highmore said.

"And the railroad," Dix said.

"Louie, why didn't you tell the sheriff this before now?" Dix said.

"Nobody asked me and then I forgot," Louie said. "I only remembered when I overheard the sheriff talking to his deputy outside the stable a little while ago. I fog up sometimes when I'm drinking."

"Louie, would you testify to this is court?:

Dix said.

"I don't have the clothes to appear in court," Louie said.

"We'll take care of that, Louie," Dix said. "Would you care for another drink?"

"Well, maybe just one more," Louie said. "A little one."

"I'll be leaving for Texas in the morning, Sheriff," Dix said. "Make sure nothing happens to Louie."

"We'll take good care of him," Highmore said.

Dix and Highmore were having a drink at the hotel bar.

"Good. He might be the defining factor at the trial," Dix said.

"Well, Mr. Dix, come say goodbye in the morning," Highmore said.

"I'll buy you breakfast," Dix said.

"I'll let you," Highmore said.

Chapter Fifty-Seven

Trixie went about her chores after Pickford left for court. She washed dishes, changed linens, did some laundry and at two o'clock, went to the post office. The Judge received more mail than anyone she ever met.

Mixed in with the mail was a telegram for her from Dix. She hurried to the café where Angel was waiting for her at their regular table.

"There you are," Angel said.

Trixie set all the mail on the chair beside the one she sat in and said, "I was at the post office."

"I see that," Angel said. "Any news from Dix."

"I got a telegram, but I didn't open it yet."

"Well go ahead and open it," Angel said.

Trixie fished out the telegram and tore open the envelope and read it quickly. Dix left Tucson and was on his way to Texas. He didn't know how long he would be there and suggested that she and the Judge take a ride to Carson City to check the progress on the house.

"Want to take a trip?" Trixie said.

"To?"

"Nevada to check on the house."

"Marty would never let me go that long," Angel said.

"To hell with Marty," Trixie said.

"When the time comes I'll tell him that very thing," Angel said. "But for now I don't want him suspecting a thing."

"I understand," Trixie said.

"Let's get some pie," Angel said.

The ride to San Antonio, Texas from Tucson was scheduled for sixteen hours. The train left at noon and would arrive at six in the morning, so Dix reserved a sleeper car so he could get some sleep along the way.

He had a large breakfast with Sheriff Highmore, skipped lunch and finished reading Black Beauty in his sleeper car. At six, he went to the dining car for supper and returned to the sleeper car by seven-thirty.

Dix rolled a cigarette, sat in the chair and thought about Louie, the town drunk who could swing the tide in favor of a guilty verdict against Valdez.

Dix knew the Pecos River. It was a thousand winding miles long and merged with the Rio Grande along the Mexican border.

Where the Pecos and Rio Grande merged wasn't that large of an area, but large enough for a man to hide in for a very long time.

Then there was the border. If Valdez went south into Mexico, he could disappear forever. He was born an American citizen, but who would care south of the border? He would blend in with every other Mexican just trying to get by.

Did didn't think Valdez would run to Mexico. He probably had strong family ties and friends in the area who would protect him.

Like he told Cohan, it wasn't going to be easy smoking him out, but for twenty-five-thousand and the chance to start the ranch free and clear, it was a job he just had to do.

The train rolled into a water stop. Dix went outside for some fresh air. He rolled a cigarette and smoked while watching the engineer load water. It reminded him of his time spent working for the railroad, long before he met Trixie.

After the water was loaded, Dix returned to his sleeper car, quit thinking about Valdez and went to sleep and woke up at five in the morning.

At six o'clock, he was in San Antonio.

Chapter Fifty-Eight

The sun wasn't up when Dix walked from the station into San Antonio. A few people were about, shopkeepers mostly, sweeping the wood sidewalks in front of their stores.

A café was reading to open. Dix tied his horse to a post, rolled a cigarette and sat on the elevated wood sidewalk to wait. By six-thirty, the sun was up and people were starting to appear on the streets.

San Antonio was a cowboy town and people got an early start to the day. At seven o'clock, the café opened and Dix went in and had eggs, bacon, potatoes and coffee for breakfast.

By eight o'clock, the town was alive and kicking. Dix went to a large general store and purchased two weeks' worth of supplies, loaded them on his horse and rode southwest out of San Antonio.

It was a four-day ride to the area called Eagle Pass where Valdez was known to have family and friends. He could hide out indefinitely from the law because they would shield him.

He would also be using another name by now.

Dix rode until noon, then stopped to rest his horse for one hour. He didn't bother with a fire. He had fresh biscuits from the general store and ate two with some water, then rolled a cigarette.

His horse kept busy munching Texas grass.

Around one o'clock, Dix was back in the saddle. He rode until dark without seeing another person, but that was to be expected as he wasn't traveling on a main road.

He built a fire and put on a stew made with fresh meat, potatoes and carrots. While his supper cooked, he tended to his horse.

After dark, the temperature cooled off, but was still warm enough so that he didn't need an overnight fire.

With Cohan's twenty-five-thousand, he would have close to fifty-thousand in the bank. He could buy five-hundred head and a couple of bulls for around ten-thousand and have enough left to hire two hands the first year. Maybe three?

With mild winters and if the bulls did their job, he could have a hundred new calves the next spring.

The following year, with a hundred more, the ranch could turn a profit of maybe twelve-thousand-dollars.

With enough profit, he could buy another five-thousand acres and increase the size of the herd.

It was a nice thought to fall asleep to.

"Dix wants me to check on the progress of the house," Trixie said to Pickford over breakfast.

"I think that's a grand idea," Pickford said.

"You do?"

"Dix knows he'll be away for several weeks and is relying on you to take care of things," Pickford said.

"I've never really had anybody rely on me before," Trixie said. "Not really. Not like this."

"Then go and take care of business," Pickford said. "It's what Dix wants."

"Alone?"

"Actually, I want to talk to the governor about a position in the state court," Pickford said. "I might as well go with you."

"When?"

"Day after tomorrow," Pickford said.

■ ■ ■ ■

Dix had a tin of a dozen eggs and he made a breakfast of three fried eggs with bacon, two biscuits and coffee. The large breakfast carried him through until supper. He stopped once in the early afternoon to rest his horse and he ate two biscuits with water. At sunset, he made a fire and put on a supper of beans, bacon, coffee and two biscuits.

While supper cooked, Dix tended to his horse.

The horse nervously twitched and snorted. "Easy, boy. I see him," Dix said.

Dix tied the horse to a tree branch and then went and stood behind a tree with his Colt drawn and waited.

"Hello to camp," a man said from the dark.

"Hello yourself," Dix said.

"I smelled your coffee," the man said.

"Come by the fire where I can see you and pour yourself a cup," Dix said.

The man slowly walked his horse into camp to the fire. The horse wasn't much and the man less. He was about nineteen or so, unarmed, thin and dressed in clothes that had seen better days.

Dix walked to the fire and holstered his Colt.

"When did you last eat?" Dix said.

"What day is it?" the man said.

"There's a sack of grain in my gear over there," Dix said. "Give your horse a pound and then fix a plate of food."

Dix sat and filled a plate and ate beside the fire. The man dug out the grain and gave it to his horse. "I'm obliged to you, mister," he said.

"Grab a plate and eat," Dix said. "Grab one of those biscuits, too."

The man fixed a plate, sat beside Dix and started to eat. "You're a good cook, mister . . . ?" the man said.

"Dix."

"Hardy. Thomas Joseph Hardy. My folks just call me TJ."

"Well, Thomas Joseph Hardy, what are you doing wandering around with no food, guns or grain for your horse?" Dix said.

"Bout a week ago, I left Dallas for the Pecos to meet up with my pa," Hardy said. "We got us a small place outside of Dallas, but it's just me and ma run it. Pa's in the army, you see. I'm supposed to pick up six horses he bought from the army and bring them home. Anyway, two nights ago these three men ride into my camp as friendly as can be. We shared grub and a pint of whiskey and played cards. The next morning. When I woke up, everybody was pointing their guns cept me. Took everything I had but my canteen. They didn't kill me, though, which I thought right considerate of them."

"Have another plate of food and a biscuit," Dix said. "You can ride along with me to the Pecos."

Hardy fixed another plate of food. "Mr. Dix, what is that badge you're wearing? Are you some kind of lawman?"

"Federal Warrant Officer," Dix said. "I work for the federal court. My job is to bring in wanted outlaws."

"Sounds like a dangerous job," Hardy said.

"No more dangerous than breaking horses," Dix said. "Do you like peaches? I got some canned peaches and a hankering for some."

"I could eat some peaches," Hardy said.

Dix grinned as he reached into his gear.

Chapter Fifty-Nine

The train left Washington DC at seven in the morning. Trixie and Pickford reserved sleeper cars and after dropping off their luggage, they met in the dining car for breakfast at eight o'clock.

"Judge, can you do something for me?" Trixie said.

As Pickford sliced into buttermilk pancakes, he said, "Ask."

"Could you teach me to play chess?"

"I didn't pack my set, but there is usually a set in the gentleman's car," Pickford said.

"The gentlemen's car?" Trixie said.

Pickford grinned. "I can borrow it," he said.

"You bring in a lot of outlaws?" Hardy said as he and dix rode along after breakfast.

"Well, I haven't kept an exact count, but around a hundred and sixty or so," Dix said.

"Are you after one now?" Hardy said. "I

mean, why else would you be out here?"

"This isn't a pleasure ride, I'll tell you that much," Dix said.

Hardy grinned. "Ma always said I talk too much," he said.

Pickford explained the object of chess and what each piece could and couldn't do on the board.

"Are you ready to play a practice game?" Pickford said.

"I think so, yes," Trixie said.

"You have white, so make the first move," Pickford said.

Around one in the afternoon, Dix and Hardy stopped to rest their horses for one hour. They allowed the horses to eat their fill of Texas grass, while they ate cans of peaches and biscuits.

"What does your pa do for the army?" Dix said.

"He's a Sergeant Major at Fort Clark down at Eagle Pass," Hardy said. "And he's done just about everything. He joined in fifty-eight, fought in the war, was assigned to reconstruction and then later worked on the railroad as security. Now he patrols the border."

"What's your pa's first name?" Dix said.

"Thomas, same as mine, only he's Thomas James instead of Thomas Joseph," Hardy said.

"The world never ceases to amaze me," Dix said. "If you're ready, let's move out."

After a practice game, Pickford and Trixie played a real game that lasted two hours. After Trixie surrendered her queen, Trixie said, "I can see why Dix always get so frustrated when he comes back from playing a game with you."

"Well, we played through lunch, care for an early dinner?" Pickford said.

"Give me five minutes to change my blouse," Trixie said.

After changing, Trixie and Pickford went to the dining car for dinner. The special was glazed ham with potatoes, carrots and rolls.

"The secret to beating Dix is to slow down the game," Pickford said. "He is a man of action and the slow pace and waiting causes him to get careless and make moves he otherwise wouldn't make."

"He's a good player though, right?" Trixie said.

"An excellent player except for that one weakness," Pickford said.

"Can we play again tomorrow?"

"As we have nothing else to do, we sure

can," Pickford said.

"I don't know why but the hairs on the back of my neck are standing up," Hardy said.

"Because we're being followed," Dix said. "Three men about a quarter mile behind us."

"Do you think it's the three who robbed me?" Hardy said.

"We'll find out soon enough," Dix said. "Let's make camp and get supper going."

"But . . ." Hardy said.

"There's a good spot under that tree," Dix said.

They made camp and built a fire. Supper was fresh meat, beans, potatoes, coffee and biscuits.

"As soon as it's dark, take my rifle and your horse and take cover in that bush over there," Dix said. "Can you make an owl sound."

"Sure."

"If it's the same men, hoot three times," Dix said. "If it's not, hoot once."

"Getting dark," Hardy said.

"Take my rifle and your horse and go," Dix said.

"But . . ."

"Now," Dix said.

Hardy took Dix's Winchester, his horse

and went behind the large bush. Dix rolled and lit a cigarette, then filled a cup with coffee.

Darkness fell. There was the sound of rustling leaves. Dix unlashed his Colt. A man's voice said, "Hello to camp."

"Hello yourself," Dix said.

"We smelled your coffee," the man said.

"Come in and have a cup if you're inclined," Dix said.

"Thanks, mister," the man said.

Dix watched as three men walked their horses into camp and stood in front of the fire.

"Coffee smells good," one of the three men said.

"Help yourself," Dix said.

"Thanks," the man said.

From the bushes, Hardy hooted three times.

"Say, you three wouldn't happen to be the men who robbed a kid and took everything he had about three nights ago?" Dix said.

"What?" the man said.

"Sure, that was you," Dix said. "Made out you were friendly and in the morning you stripped him clean."

"Mister, you're crazy," the man said.

"Hey look, he's wearing a badge," one of the other men said.

"Now you three leave what you stole from the boy and get going, or I'm taking you in," Dix said. "In the saddle or draped over it."

"Three of us and one of you, mister," the first man said.

"Three slow, liquored up trail bums," Dix said. "I'll take my chances."

"Let's kill this sum bitch and be done with him," the second man said.

"Move for your gun and I'll kill the three of you where you stand," Dix said.

The three men stared at Dix for several seconds. Then the first man reached for his gun. Dix drew his Colt, shot him and then shot the other two. It was over in three seconds.

Dix emptied the spent shells, reloaded and holstered his Colt and said, "Come on out, kid."

Hardy walked his horse out from behind the bushes. "Jesus Christ, you killed them all," he said.

"They asked for it," Dix said. "See if they still have your stuff."

Hardy went through the three dead men's gear and found his holster and gun and his Henry rifle.

"These are mine alright," Hardy said.

"Come on, kid, let's eat," Dix said.

"What about them?" Hardy said.

"We'll throw them over the saddle in the morning and bring them with us to Eagle Pass," Dix said. "Maybe the law wants them."

Dix and hardy fixed plates of food and ate around the fire.

"Mr. Dix, weren't you scared back then?" hardy said.

"You can't do what I do and be scared, kid," Dix said. "If you are, don't wear this badge."

"Do you think they're wanted?" Hardy said.

"Most likely," Dix said. "That's why they were so quick to go for their guns."

"I'd like you to meet my pa," Hardy said.

"Looking forward to it," Dix said.

Chapter Sixty

Trixie and Pickford rode to the ranch in a rented buggy. Pickford handled the reins. Trixie didn't know what to expect and felt a bit lost without Dix, but she kept quiet about it to Pickford.

When they arrived at the sight, Trixie was a bit shocked at the progress the work crews, led by Thomas Mitchell, had made.

A crew of six were framing the house, while another crew of four was framing the bunkhouse a hundred yards to the right.

Pickford helped Trixie dismount the buggy and Mitchell broke away from the crews and approached them.

"Mr. Dix, a pleasant surprise to see you again," Mitchell said.

"Mr. Mitchell, this is my friend Judge Pickford," Trixie said.

Mitchell shook hands with the judge. "A pleasure, sir. Mrs. Dix, come check the progress," Mitchell said.

They toured the house and bunkhouse and Mitchell sought Trixie's approval in each room, the structure, the wells and grounds. With a sudden air of confidence, Trixie reviewed the plans and approved of the progress, which pleased Mitchell greatly.

"The barn and corral will begin work as soon as the bunkhouse is finished," Mitchell said. "The house, of course, is more detailed work."

"Mr. Mitchell, the bunkhouse will be what color paint?" Trixie said.

"The plans call for gray," Mitchell said.

Trixie walked to the table where the blueprints were located. Mitchell and Pickford followed her.

Trixie looked at the blueprint for the bunkhouse. "Do you see all the trim around the windows and doors?" she said. "Do you think white paint on the trim might brighten things up a bit?"

"I do," Mitchel said. "It shall be so."

"Good," Trixie said.

"Suggestions for the house, Mrs. Dix?" Mitchell said.

Pickford looked at Trixie and grinned.

Eagle Pass wasn't much of a settlement along the Pecos River. Just a few hundred people at most and every one of them watched as Dix and Hardy rode in with the three dead outlaws in tow.

"Is there a place to bury these three outlaws?" Dix said.

"We got us a cemetery, but nobody is going to bury them for free," a man said.

"I'll pay five dollars a man and you can keep whatever you find in their gear," Dix said. "And you can keep the horses."

Some men walked the horses toward the cemetery.

"TJ, how far to Fort Scott?" Dix said.

"An hour."

"Lead the way."

An hour later, Hardy and Dix reached Fort Scott Army Outpost, home to two hundred soldiers that primarily patrolled the border. The gates were open and soldiers were stationed out front.

"Thomas Hardy to see Sergeant Major Hardy," Hardy told the soldiers.

A few minutes later, Hardy and Dix waited outside the commanding officer's office. Sergeant Major Hardy, a tall and stout man in his forties exited the office and smiled at his son.

"Good to see you son," sergeant Major Hardy said.

"Pa, this man . . ." TJ said.

"Well I'll be a son of a bitch," Sergeant

Major Hardy said. "Lieutenant Dix as I live and breathe."

"Pa, you know Mr. Dix?" TJ said.

"He was my lieutenant on the railroad," Sergeant Major Hardy said. "How on earth did you two link up?"

"Can a man get a cup of coffee around here?" Dix said.

It wasn't dinner time, but Sergeant Major Hardy was able to convince the cooks to brew up a pot of coffee and they sat at a table in the mess hall to drink it. Hardy told his father what Dix had done for him on the trail and Sergeant Major Hardy said, "No surprise to me son, Dix was the best officer I ever served under."

Sergeant Major Hardy looked at the badge on Dix's chest. "I'd be willing to wager you're not here to swim in the Pecos," he said.

"Actually, I'm after a murderer," Dix said. "His name is Robert Valdez and he breaks horses."

"Who did he murder?" Sergeant Major Hardy said.

"A boy about TJ's age," Dix said. "In Tucson about seven months ago. He's from here and this is where he will come to hide."

"You think he's busting horses for the army?" Sergeant Major Hardy said. "We have three men for that job. Two are Irishmen. The third is named Lopez."

Dix took out the photograph and showed it to Sergeant Major Hardy. The look on his face told Dix that Lopez was Valdez.

"Where is he?" Dix said.

"Son, go find Sergeant O'Brien," Sergeant Major Hardy said.

"Yes, Pa," TJ said.

After TJ left the mess hall, Sergeant Major Hardy said, "Why did he murder this boy?"

"Nobody knows but him," Dix said. "What I can tell you is he beat the boy to death and it took two days for him to die."

"My God," Sergeant Major Hardy said.

After a few minutes, TJ returned with Sergeant O'Brien. "You've picked up horses from Lopez?" Sergeant Major Hardy said.

"Only last week, why?" Sergeant O'Brien said.

"Let's go see the Colonel," Sergeant Major Hardy said.

Colonel Tweed read the warrant and then said, "This is sad news indeed."

"Colonel, shall I form an escort party for Mr. Dix?' Sergeant Major Hardy said.

"I appreciate that, but that would only alert him and give him the chance to run," Dix said.

"I'm afraid he's right," Tweed said.

"Colonel, can you put me up for tonight?" Dix said.

"Sergeant Major, show Mr. Dix a room in our guest quarters," Tweed said. "And you'll dine with me at my table at seven tonight. Sergeant Major, you and your son will sit at my table as well."

"You handled yourself very well today," Pickford said. He and Trixie were having dinner at the Carson City Hotel restaurant.

"I was nervous," Trixie said. "Most men don't like taking orders from women."

"Times are changing, dear," Pickford said. "In Wyoming, women have the right to vote. Women own businesses and work jobs and do pretty much what men do. In twenty years, who knows what women will be capable of."

"Do you think so?" Trixie said.

"I know so," Pickford said. "And I'll tell you something else. Had Dix been here today every man working would have paid him his due respect, but he wasn't there and the respect they showed you was earned, not given."

"I think we're going to enjoy living here," Trixie said.

"And that reminds me," Pickford said. "In

the morning, I have to see the governor before we leave about my appointment to the state court."

"Are you going to miss Washington?" Trixie said.

"Like I'd miss a pebble in my shoe," Pickford said.

TJ told Colonel Tweed about the encounter with the three outlaws and his father looked at Dix.

"It doesn't surprise me at all," Sergeant Major Hardy said. "For four years Lieutenant Dix fought outlaws, bandits, thieves and Indians and saved our bacon on more than one occasion."

"Mr. Dix, it appears that you have more than one admirer," Tweed said.

"Those days were a long time ago," Dix said. "In fact, I'm retiring after this job. My wife and I bought a little ranch in Nevada. We're going to raise cattle."

"That's grand," Sergeant Major Hardy said. "Just grand."

"Mr. Dix, may I suggest a drink in my quarters after supper?" Tweed said. "Sergeant Major, you're invited as well."

"That is also grand, sir," Sergeant Major Hardy said.

Chapter Sixty-One

"I'd feel better if you allowed me to come along," Sergeant Major Hardy said. "It's the least I can do for saving my son's life."

"Not necessary," Dix said. "He's a good boy. You raised him well."

"Watch your back," Sergeant Major Hardy said. "A cornered man is a dangerous man."

"Will you be back?" TJ said.

"Most likely," Dix said.

"I'll keep a seat for you in the mess hall," Sergeant Major Hardy said.

Dix rode out of Fort Scott and headed south along the Pecos River. According to Sergeant O'Brien, Valdez had a small place about twelve miles south and one mile east of the river.

He rode at an easy pace. It was a hot morning and there was no sense working his horse into a lather. O'Brien had said that if he turned east after twelve miles and rode another mile, he would come upon the

Valdez place. There was a house, barn and a large corral for breaking horses. There was more than one family living there. Most likely, Valdez's relatives.

Relatives were a problem. They would defend him and protect him and Dix didn't want to have to kill innocent people.

O'Brien said there was a bend in the river that marked twelve miles. Dix reached the bend and dismounted. "Go eat some grass if you want to," he told the horse.

Dix found a shady spot under a tree that faced the river, sat and rolled a cigarette. He smoked watching the river flow past him.

He didn't want to kill innocent people. He didn't even want to kill Valdez if it could be avoided. He wanted the man so stand trial for his crime and be punished by the law, not the gun.

Cigarette spent, Dix stood and walked to his horse. "Let's get to it," he said and mounted the saddle.

He headed east and rode about a mile and spotted chimney smoke before the house. Dix continued riding until he was three hundred yards from the house and stopped and took out his binoculars.

Two men were working with a horse in the corral. Neither of them was Valdez. A woman was on the porch, shucking corn.

Dix rode right up to the corral and dismounted. The two Mexican men onside the corral walked over to Dix.

"Speak English?" Dix said.

"Yes," one of the men said.

"Do you know what this badge means?" Dix said and tapped the badge on his chest.

"Yes," the other man said. "The law."

"I'm looking for Robert Valdez," Dix said. "And don't bother to tell me he isn't here, I've already been to the army and I know he breaks horses for them."

The two men stared at Dix.

"Are you related to him?" Dix said.

"I am his cousin," the first man said.

"I am his brother," the second man said.

"Now listen to me the both of you," Dix said. "He has to answer for what's he's done in a court of law and it's my job to bring him to that court. I will not tolerate any interference. Is that understood?"

"We understand," the cousin said.

"Is he in the house?" Dix said.

"No," the brother said.

"Where is he?" Dix said.

"You won't kill him?" the cousin said.

"I will do everything I can to bring him in peacefully," Dix said.

"He is with his wife in a little cabin a mile

to the west," the brother said. "He takes the troubled horses there to work with them."

"And his wife Maria is with him?" Dix said.

"Yes."

"If you lied to me, I will come back with forty soldiers," Dix said.

"We didn't lie," the brother said. "He is there."

Dix mounted the saddle and rode west. After a mile or so, he came to the little cabin where a horse was in the corral. He dismounted at the corral and said, "Horse, wait right here."

Drawing his Colt, Dix walked to the cabin and stopped at the porch steps.

"This is Federal Warrant Officer Dix and I have a warrant for the arrest of Robert Valdez," Dix said. "Come out with your hands up and there won't be any trouble."

The screen door opened and Maria slowly walked out to the porch. She was at least seven months pregnant.

"Mrs. Valdez?" Dix said.

"Yes."

"Where is your husband?"

"He went hunting," Maria said.

"How long ago?" Dix said.

Maria didn't respond.

"How long ago?" Dix said.

"Robert is a good man," Maria said.

"I'm sure he is," Dix said. "But he killed a boy and has to answer for that."

Maria walked down the stairs. "You don't understand," she said.

"Mrs. Valdez, when will he be back?" Dix said.

"Please, please, you don't understand," Maria said.

"I understand that he beat a nineteen-year-old boy to death," Dix said. "Now where is he?"

Crying, Maria slumped to her knees in front of Dix. "That nineteen-year-old boy raped me," she said.

"What?" Dix said.

"This is his baby I carry," Maria said.

"How do you know that?" Dix said.

"Bob was kicked in the privates by a horse he was training," Maria said. "He can still function, but no more babies the doctor say."

Dix took Maria's shoulders and lifted her to his feet.

"Bob snapped," Maria said. "He didn't mean . . ."

"To kill the boy," Valdez said from behind the Dix.

Dix turned around. Valdez was unarmed and appeared defeated.

"I lost my head," Valdez said. :It wasn't until later that I realized what I had done."

"Why did you run?" Dix said.

"The Cohan family is rich and white," Valdez said. "I am Mexican and poor."

"Oh, Jesus Christ," Dix said.

"Maria, I will go back with Mr. Dix and stand trial," Valdez said.

"No, Robert. Please," Maria said.

"I can promise you a fair and honest trial," Dix said.

Valdez nodded.

"I am going with you," Maria said.

"That would be good," Dix said.

"I'll hitch the wagon," Valdez said.

"This is my son Peter," Valdez said. "My brother Jose and my cousin Canelo and his wife Isolina."

"Sit and have a plate of food with us," Maria said.

"Jose, will you get the wagon ready with supplies," Valdez said. "We have a long journey ahead of us."

Dix sat next to Valdez.

"What will happen to my brother?" Jose said.

"That will be up to a judge, but when all the facts come to light, I don't think it will add up to much," Dix said.

"I will get the wagon ready," Jose said.

"Well I'll be damned," Sergeant Major Hardy said.

"Sergeant Major, have a quest quarters prepared for Mr. and Mrs. Valdez," Colonel Tweed said.

"I am not a prisoner?" Valdez said.

"No," Tweed said. "Have your wife get some rest. We serve dinner at six-thirty. You will dine at my table."

"Thank you, Colonel," Valdez said.

"Come with me and I'll show you to your quarters," Sergeant Major Hardy said to Valdez and Maria.

After Valdez and Maria left with Sergeant Major Hardy, Tweed removed a bottle of whiskey from a desk drawer and filled two shot glasses. "By God, after that story, I could use a drink," he said and handed a glass to Dix.

"Thanks, Colonel," Dix said.

"What do you think will happen to him?" Tweed said.

"I really can't say," Dix said. "I'm not the court. But I'll tell you this much, I'll do whatever I can to help them. God knows they need it."

Tweed sipped his drink. "God knows," he said.

Chapter Sixty-Two

Before leaving San Antonio. Dix sent a telegram to Judge Pickford asking him to wire Cohan in New York City, requesting he meet them in Pickford's court.

The ride from San Antonio to Washington was scheduled for twenty hours and Dix reserved two sleeper cars. The train left at ten o'clock in the evening and was scheduled to arrive at six PM.

Maria was exhausted from the long ride in the wagon and from carrying the burden of the baby and slept most of the trip.

Valdez brought Maria breakfast and lunch to the sleeper car and rarely left her side.

Dix spent most of his time in his sleeper car, reading a book and thinking about his ranch.

In Washington, Dix walked his horse to the courthouse, while Valdez and Maria took a taxi.

Dix escorted them into the courthouse and told them to wait on the bench outside Pickford's chambers. Then he entered the chambers where Pickford and Cohan waited.

Cohan rushed to Dix and shook his hand. "You have done a man's job, sir," Cohan said.

"If you'll just hold on a moment, Mr. Cohan," Dix said, opened the door and said, "Maria?"

Maria entered the chambers and closed the door.

"Judge, Mr. Cohan, this is Maria Valdez, Robert's wife," Dix said.

"Where is Robert?" Cohan said.

"Don't worry, he's right outside," Dix said. "Maria, tell Judge Pickford what happened."

Maria approached Pickford's desk. "A few days a week I worked for Miss Orr's dress shop, helping her make dresses," she said. "I work late one night on a dress. Bob waited for me at the café up the street. Andy, he bothered me before, but I didn't see him in the alleyway next to the shop. He grabbed me and take me around back where it is dark and he raped me."

"That's a lie," Cohan shouted.

Maria looked at Cohan. "This is his baby

I carry," she said.

"That's a lie," Cohan shouted.

"Robert was kicked in the testicles by a horse he was training," Dix said. "No more children for him. I wired the doctor in Tucson for the medical report."

"Bob found out what Andy do and Bob lost his head," Maria said. "That's why Bob killed your son."

Cohan looked at Pickford. "I have the medical report right here," he said. "Valdez couldn't have fathered that child."

"She is carrying your grandchild, Mr. Cohan," Dix said. "What are you going to do about it?"

Cohan stepped backward and slumped into a chair. Pickford went to the small bar in the corner of the room and poured a shot of whiskey and brought it to Cohan. "James," Pickford said.

Cohan took the drink. "Where is Mr. Valdez?" he said.

Dix opened the door. "Bob?" he said.

Valdez entered the chambers and looked at Cohan. "I am very sorry about Andy," Valdez said. "Very sorry."

Cohan nodded and then burst into tears.

Dix walked to Pickford, who had returned to the bar and poured two shots of whiskey. He handed one to Dix. "I'd say James was right," he said. "You've done a man's job, sir."

Chapter Sixty-Three

"We leave for Tucson in the morning," Dix said.

Dix, Trixie and Pickford were having dinner in the dining room.

"I wrote an opinion to give the judge in Tucson," Pickford said. "Along with the medical report and your testimony, it should carry some weight."

"How long will you be gone?" Trixie said.

"A week," Dix said. "Then we can head out to Nevada and check on things. Mr. Cohan is a man of his word and paid me twenty-five-thousand, so this is my last job. Judge, what about you?"

"The governor approved my appointment to the state superior court," Pickford said. "It's not Washington, but I've had enough of Washington."

"I can't imagine what that woman has gone through," Trixie said.

"People endure what they have to," Pickford said. "It's all that we can do and survive."

After dinner, Dix and Pickford took brandy on the back porch where the air was much cooler.

Dix rolled and lit a cigarette.

"You should have seen Trixie take control," Pickford said. "She is a woman to be admired and cherished."

"I do on both accounts," Dix said.

"When you return from Tucson, will you go to Nevada right away?" Pickford said.

"I expect so," Dix said.

"It will take me about a month to fully clear my cases and to sell the house," Pickford said.

"By then the house will be livable," Dix said.

"Why are you here talking to an old man?" Pickford said. "Your wife is waiting."

Dix watched Trixie brush her hair before bed.

"What's going to happen to them?" Trixie said.

"I can't say for sure, but I expect leniency," Dix said.

"You'll be gone a week?"

"At least."

Trixie set the brush aside and walked to the bed. "Come make it up to me," she said. "In advance."

Chapter Sixty-Four

The ride to Tucson took forty-eight hours by train. Maria and Valdez spent most of their time in their sleeper car.

Dix and Cohan played chess in the gentlemen's car when Dix wasn't in his sleeper car reading a book.

James Jr. and Michael met Cohan, Dix, Valdez and Maria at the station in Tucson.

"We never expected this, Pa," James Jr. said.

"Nobody did, but it's a situation that needs to be dealt with," Cohan said. "Boys, I'll be saying in town tonight. Meet me in court at ten o'clock tomorrow morning."

"Yes, Pa," James Jr. said.

Everybody in town stared at them as they walked to the Tucson Hotel where the sheriff met them in the lobby.

"Mr. Valdez, I'm not putting you in jail, but you are under house arrest," the sheriff said. "Do you understand what that means?"

"Yes," Valdez said. "I'm not to leave the hotel."

"A deputy will be posted in the lobby until morning at which time you will be escorted to the courthouse," the sheriff.

"Robert, we'll see you for dinner around six," Dix said.

Trixie and Pickford had just sat down to dinner when there was a knock on the door. "It must be the delivery from the store," Trixie said.

She went to the door and opened it. To her surprise, it was Angel.

"Angel, what are you . . . ?" Trixie said.

Marty stepped around Angle and aimed a Schofield .44 revolver at Trixie. "Inside," he said. "Now."

Trixie backed up. Angel closed the door.

"Marty, what do you think you're doing?" Trixie said.

"Where's the judge?" Marty said.

"Kitchen," Trixie said.

"Move," Marty said.

Trixie, Marty and Angel entered the kitchen. At the table, Pickford stood up.

"What is the meaning of this?" Pickford said.

Marty cocked the Schofield and aimed it

at Pickford. "Sit down. Shut up," he said.

"I'll do no such thing," Pickford said.

Marty put the Schofield to Trixie's head. "No?" he said.

Pickford took his chair.

"Angel find something to tie up the judge with," Marty said. "You, Trixie, sit down."

Trixie took a chair at the table.

"What do you want?" Pickford said.

"You're not very bright there, judge, are you?" Marty said. "What do you think we want? We want money."

Trixie glared at Angel.

"Sorry, honey, it's just the way things are," Angel said.

"Now then, to business," Marty said. "Angel says you have close to fifty-thousand-dollars. That's what it's going to cost to save your lives."

"You fool," Pickford said. "That money is in the bank and only Dix can get it and he's in Tucson."

"She can get it," Marty said.

"No, I can't," Trixie said.

Marty slapped Trixie and she fell to the floor.

"Was that necessary" Angel said as she helped Trixie stand up.

"I told you to tie him up," Marty said.

Angel went through the kitchen cabinets

and found some heavy twine. She cut some with a knife and tied Pickford's hands to the chair.

'Now then," Marty said. "The money.'

"I told you, the money is in the bank and only Dix can withdraw it," Pickford said.

Marty walked to Pickford and punched him in the face, knocking him and the chair to the floor.

Trixie rushed to Pickford. "Judge?" she said.

"I say it again, I want the money," Marty said.

"And I'll tell you again, only Dix can . . ." Pickford said and Marty kicked him in the ribs with his shoe.

Trixie jumped up and slapped Marty. "You animal," she said.

Marty slapped her hard across the face and she fell next to Pickford. He went to the kitchen counter and picked up a sharp, bread knife.

"Every time you lie to me, I'm cutting some shit off you," Marty said.

"Is Maria alright?" Dix said.

"Yes. She us resting: Valdez said. "I will have food brought to our room a bit later."

"Mr. Valdez, I want you to know that however this goes in court tomorrow, the baby will be taken care of," Cohan said.

"Mr. Cohan, I took the life of your son and I am sorry for that," Valdez said. "But the baby is . . ."

"My grandson," Cohan said. "And half his blood in mine. You must allow me to help in any way that I can."

Valdez looked at Dix.

"He's right, Robert," Dix said. "As the grandfather, he has the right to help the baby have a good life."

"We will talk about it after we see the judge in the morning," Valdez said.

"Fair enough," Cohan said.

"Now, where is the money, honey?" Marty said.

"I told you, in the bank and only Dix can get it," Pickford said.

"Untie his left hand," Marty said.

Angel untied Pickford's left hand.

"Put your left hand on the table," Marty said.

Pickford stared at Marty. Then he cocked the Schofield and put it against Trixie's head. She gasped and closed her eyes.

Pickford placed his left hand on the table. Marty lowered the Schofield and placed the bread knife just behind the fingernail of Pickford's pinky.

"Now I ask again, the money," Marty said.

"And I'll say it again, only Dix can get it," Pickford said.

Marty sliced down hard and severed Pickford's pinky at the nail. Pickford screamed as blood gushed from the wound.

"Angel, tie it up," Marty said.

Angel grabbed a dish towel and wrapped it around Pickford's pinky.

Marty placed the Schofield against Trixie's head. This time she kept her eyes open and glared at Marty.

"Alright, Judge, last chance," Marty said. "I don't like what I hear and I blow this bitch's brains all over this nice, pretty table. The money."

"Wait," Pickford said. "Just wait."

Marty lowered the Schofield. "Go on," he said.

"It's true what I said about the bank, but I have money in the house," Pickford said. "It's yours if you'll just leave."

"How much?"

"Twenty-thousand."

"Twenty-thousand?" Marty said.

"In cash. It's yours if you just leave," Pickford said.

"Where is it?" Marty said.

"In my safe in the study," Pickford said.

"Cut him loose," Marty said.

Angel used the knife to free Pickford's right hand. Marty removed a smaller revolver from a pocket and gave it to Angel. "If he makes one false move, shoot him," he said. "Judge, even if you live, she won't," Marty said and nodded at Trixie.

"Let's go, Judge," Angel said.

Pickford stood, holding the bloody towel over his left hand. He and Angel walked to his study.

Marty looked at Trixie. "You should have never left, Trixie," he said. "A person has to know where they belong and you belong in the gutter with me."

"You go to hell," Trixie said.

Mart went to the stove and filled a cup with coffee, then returned to Trixie. He touched her hair. "I always wondered what all the fuss was about under that dress," he said. "Why every bean wiggler with a five-dollar-piece wanted you first."

"Don't you touch me," Trixie said.

Marty laughed, then sipped some coffee.

Angel and Pickford returned. Angel had a small briefcase and set it on the table. Marty looked inside. "Twenty-thousand?" he said.

"I counted it," Angel said. "Now let's get out of here."

"Tie him up," Marty said. "Hands and ankles. Tight."

"Sit," Angel said and Pickford took his chair.

Angel grabbed the twine and tied Pickford's wrists and ankles to the chair.

Marty grabbed Trixie by the hair and yanked her to her feet. "Let's find out what all the fuss was about," he said.

"Marty, we didn't come here for that," Angel said.

"You didn't. I did," Marty said. "Let's go, sweetheart."

Trixie looked at Pickford. "Courage," he said.

"Yeah, courage," Marty said and he dragged her to a bedroom and slammed the door.

"I didn't know he was going to do that," Angel said.

From behind the closed bedroom door, there was the sound of a slap and a cry.

"He doesn't know what he's just done," Pickford said. "Do you know who Dix is, what he is?"

"Be quiet," Angel said.

"Dix is the Four Horsemen of the Apocalypse rolled into one," Pickford said. "There won't be any place you can run to he won't find you and when he does, even God couldn't stop him."

"Shut up," Angel said.

"One question," Pickford said. "What are you going to do when the man comes around?"

Pickford could see the panic is Angel's eyes. "I told you to shut up," Angel said.

"Sure, I'll shut up," Pickford said. "But that won't save you. Nothing will."

"I'll put a bullet in you, old man," Angel said.

Marty emerged from the bedroom. "Let's go," he said and grabbed the briefcase from the table.

"Remember what I said," Pickford said.

Marty punched Pickford in the face, knocking him and the chair to the floor. Pickford was unconscious for a few minutes and when he woke up, a battered and bruised Trixie was cutting the twine around his wrists.

"Trixie," he said.

She cut the twine around his legs and helped him stand up. He looked at her face. Her left eye was closed. Her lips were swollen and bloody. Red marks were on her neck. He dress was soaked with blood.

"Sit down," Pickford said.

"Your finger," Trixie said.

"The bleeding has stopped," Pickford said as he sat Trixie into a chair.

"Wait here," Pickford said.

He rushed out of the house and ran to the house at the end of the street where Doctor Edmund lived with his wife.

Pickford pounded on the door. Mary, Edmund's wife opened the door. "Judge?" she said.

"Tell Edmund to grab his bag and get over to my house immediately," Pickford said.

Edmund entered Pickford's study, where he was in a chair, having a glass of whiskey. "Let me see that finger," Edmund said.

"The bleeding stopped," Pickford said.

Edmund cleaned the wound, then wrapped it in clean gauze.

"How is she?" Pickford said.

"Her face will heal," Edmund said. "Mary is giving her a bath. Alan, she was one month pregnant. I doubt she even knew."

"Oh God," Pickford said. "Can she . . . ?"

"Have more? Yes."

"Thank God for that," Pickford said.

"Alan, I could use a drink," Edmund said. "A big one."

Chapter Sixty-Five

The honorable Judge McCoy presided over the hearing. Valdez, Maria, Cohan, his two sons, the sheriff and Dix were present in the closed courtroom.

Valdez waived his right to a jury.

"I have heard all the evidence and facts, statements from Mr. Valdez, Mr. Dix and Mr. Cohan and read the opinion from the honorable Judge Pickford," McCoy said. "And while I agree that Mr. Valdez didn't mean to kill Andrew Cohan, he did indeed, kill him. Mr. Valdez, please stand and face the bench."

Valdez stood and faced McCoy.

"Mr. Valdez, taking into account all circumstances, I sentence you to ten years for the . . ." McCoy said.

Cohan jumped to his feet. "Your honor," he said. "As a defense attorney I must protest such a sentence."

"Sit down, Mr. Cohan," McCoy said.

"Now then, as I was saying. I sentence you to ten years for the crime of murder, of which nine years is suspended. The remaining year will be spent under house arrest at the Cohan ranch breaking horses, if there are no objections. Are there?"

"No, your honor, no objections," Cohan said.

"James Jr., Michael?" McCoy said.

"None, your honor," James Jr. said.

"To continue," McCoy said. "After one year at house arrest, Mr. Valdez, you will be free to go about your business."

McCoy banged his gavel. "Case dismissed.

"I'll be a son of a bitch," Dix said.

Dix and Cohan had a drink at a saloon before Dix caught the train home.

"Life is a very strange thing, Mr. Dix," Cohan said. "I came to you with vengeance in my heart and walked away with a grandchild."

"After the one year?" Dix said.

"I have some land on the ranch not in use at the moment," Cohan said. "It's perfect for a house and a place to break horses."

Dix smiled. "Good luck, to all of you," he said.

"And you," Cohan said. "And now that

you've officially retired, you're off to your ranch."

"Just as soon as I get home," Dix said.

Chapter Sixty-Six

Dix walked to the Judge's house with his horse in tow. He stopped at the front porch, where Pickford sat with a drink of whiskey.

Dix walked up to the porch and looked at the bandage on Pickford's left pinky.

"Something's happened," Dix said. "What?"

Pickford picked up the bottle of whiskey and filled a second glass. "Sit. Have a drink and I'll tell you," he said.

Dix and Pickford entered the bedroom where Trixie was asleep.

"Trixie, honey, Dix is home," Pickford said.

Her eyes wasn't as swollen and her lips not as puffy and she opened her eyes and looked up at Dix. "I lost our baby," she said, sat up and cried as Dix held her tight.

■ ■ ■ ■

"I want a warrant for each of them," Dix said.

"In the morning," Pickford said.

Dix and Pickford had returned to the porch for another drink. Dix rolled and lit a cigarette. "Make them wanted dead or alive," Dix said.

"Robbery, assault and battery and rape doesn't warrant a dead or alive warrant," Pickford said.

"They killed our unborn child," Dix said. "That's murder, isn't it?"

"Alright, but if at all possible, I'd like to try them in my court and sentence him to hang," Pickford said.

"And her?"

"Twenty to life."

"You'll do the warrants in the morning?"

"First thing," Pickford said. "Right now I have to prepare some dinner for Trixie."

"I'll do it," Dix said. "That finger must be killing you."

Dix prepared a hearty chicken soup, salad and steaks for himself and Pickford. Trixie claimed her jaw was still too sore for red meat.

Trixie was mostly silent and kept her head down. Finally, she spoke and said, "You'll be going after them?"

"Of course," Dix said.

"Start at the saloon," Trixie said. "The other bartender, his name is Parker, he'll know where they went."

"I was going there anyway," Dix said.

"Don't kill him," Trixie said. "I want him to hang for what he did to our baby."

Dix nodded. "Alright," he said.

"In Judge Pickford's court," Trixie said.

"We've already discussed that," Pickford said.

"Good," Trixie said.

"There is something I want you to do for me," Dix said. "I want you and the Judge to pack up and go to Nevada. I don't know how long I'll be gone. The house should be just about finished anyway."

"That's a fine idea, Dix," Pickford said. "Trixie?"

Trixie nodded. "I never want to see Washington or anybody in it ever again." She said.

As they waited for sleep, Trixie said, "Do you still love me? I've heard stories that after a woman is . . . violated, that her man stops loving her."

"I can promise you this," Dix said. "That I will love you until the day I die."

Trixie smiled in the dark. "Good," she said. "Just don't make it anytime soon. The dying thing, I mean."

Chapter Sixty-Seven

Dix waited until after lunch with Trixie before he walked over to the saloon. At one-thirty in the afternoon, it would be packed with patrons and he wanted plenty of witnesses to back him up.

There were several senators, four or five congressmen, two judges and an assistant to the Secretary of State present in the saloon when Dix entered and walked to the bar and found a vacant space.

Parker was behind the bar. He was a tall man with a big gut who was always red in the face. He recognized Dix, but pretended that he didn't.

"Where are they?" Dix said.

"Who?"

Dix grabbed Parker by the shirt, yanked him over the bar and threw him onto a table occupied by a US Senator and two US Congressmen. The table collapsed and Parker hit the floor.

Dix held up his badge. "United Stared Federal Warrant Officer John Dixon and this man is wanted for questioning," he said.

He pinned the badge to his shirt, then pulled Parker to his feet. "I'll ask you again, where are they?" he said.

Parker stared at Dix.

"They aren't worth the beating you're about to get, nor the jail term for obstruction," Dix said.

"New Orleans," Parker said. "That's all I know."

"How do you know?" Dix said.

"He fancies himself a gambler and he's from there," Parker said. "He said he'd go back if he ever got some real money."

Dix nodded. "If you lied, you'll wish you'd never been born," he said.

"Pack everything you want to keep and leave behind what you don't," Dix said. "I'll wire my entire account to Carson City and you'll have full access to whatever you need."

"How long will you be gone?" Trixie said.

"I don't know," Dix said. "Plan on a month."

Trixie nodded. "Okay," she said. "Dix, the Judge is a very brave man. He willingly gave up his finger to save my life. He didn't hesitate for one second. He's more of a father to me than my real one ever was."

"I know that," Dix said. "And everything will work out. I'll be at the courthouse. See you for dinner."

"New Orleans," Pickford said. "Somehow I'm not surprised."

"When are you and Trixie leaving for Nevada?" Dix said.

"My leave of absence from the bench begins tomorrow," Pickford said. "If she's packed and ready, we'll leave tomorrow afternoon."

"I'll have the bank wire my account to Carson City with Trixie's name attached so she can draw funds as needed," Dix said. "Judge, you'll . . ."

"Look after her?" Pickford said. "Do you need to ask?"

"No, I suppose not," Dix said as he looked at Pickford's severed pinky.

Chapter Sixty-Eight

Dix packed the clothes he wanted to send to Nevada in one large suitcase and the clothes he wanted to bring to New Orleans in a satchel.

Trixie and Pickford packed everything they wanted to bring into several large suitcases. Pickford made arrangements with a shipping company to crate and ship his law books and files. Doctor Edmund was given the key and would give access to the shipping company. Edmund also agreed to look after Pickford's house and livery and Pickford made a gift of his buggy and horse to Edmund.

Dix went to the bank and had his account transferred to Carson City, keeping two-thousand-dollars in cash. He gave one thousand to Trixie and kept one thousand for himself.

Then they had lunch together for the last time in Pickford's home before leaving for the railroad station.

Dix hailed a large taxi for Trixie and Pickford, he rode his horse. The train to Carson City left at two o'clock. Dix's train to New Orleans left at four.

Dix waited with Trixie and Pickford until their train arrived. Trixie cried before boarding the train. Pickford shook Dix's hand.

"We will see you in Carson City," Pickford said.

"You bet," Dix said.

After their train left, Dix removed a book from his saddlebags, sat on a bench, rolled a cigarette and started to read.

Pickford knocked on Trixie's sleeper car door and said, "Trixie, it's seven o'clock, time for dinner."

Trixie opened the door. "Do I look alright?" she said.

Pickford examined her face. She had applied makeup to the fading bruise under her left eye.

"You look lovely, my dear," he said.

Trixie grinned. "You old flirt, how about a game of chess after dinner?" she said.

"Delighted," Pickford said.

Dix didn't bother with a sleeper car for the eighteen-hour ride to New Orleans. He read his book, stretched outside during water stops, had dinner at seven and continued to read the rest of the time.

He read to keep his mind from thinking about Angel and Marty. Thinking about them would fill his heart with anger and he wanted to keep this job as all others, professional.

Around midnight, he dozed for a while and woke up around five in the morning at a water stop. He stood on a platform and smoked a cigarette and watched the crew load water.

Six am was the first call for breakfast and Dix took a table and ordered pancakes with scrambled eggs and bacon.

He finished the book while he ate and left it in the gentlemen's car on the bookshelf.

The train arrived in New Orleans on time and Dix retrieved his horse and stepped onto the platform.

New Orleans was a massive city of two-hundred-thousand residents held together by levies. It was a large port town built on the Mississippi River watershed. The population was an eclectic mix of white, French, Black and mixed freed slaves.

Dix walked his horse to a small hotel on a side street that had a livery. He checked in and paid for a room for a week in advance.

He ordered up a shave and a bath and afterward, Dix took a nap until late in the afternoon. Then he dressed carefully, choosing a black shirt, black pants, his Colt and a backup .38 revolver in a shoulder holster. He chose a jacket to match the shirt and left the hotel around seven in the evening.

He started on Bourbon Street in the French Quarter, visiting saloons and cafes. Dix would order a drink, nurse it for a while as he looked around and checked out the women working as saloon girls.

By ten o'clock, Dix had visited seven establishments and decided it was time for something to eat. He stopped at a café on a side-street and ordered barbequed ribs and a mug of beer.

Music seemed to be coming from everywhere and nowhere at the same time.

After dinner, Dix continued walking the French Quarter. A uniformed police office on patrol stopped him as Dix walked along Royal Street. "Firearms are not permitted in the open in New Orleans," the police officer said.

Dix tapped his badge. "Federal Warrant Officer and I'm here on official business," he said.

"I can't hear myself think out here on the street," the police officer said. "Would you follow me please."

The police officer led Dix to the police station on Decatur Street where they talked in the lobby.

"I have a federal warrant for the arrest of Angela Wells," Dix said.

The police officer read the warrant. "Wanted for robbery, assault and murder," he said. "That's quite a lineup of charges."

"She escaped Washington and is believed to be somewhere in New Orleans," Dix said.

"New Orleans is a big town, Mr. Dix," the police officer said.

"Not so big she can hide what she is," Dix said. "She came here with a man named Martin Farrow. He fancies himself a gambler, but she's what they call out west a sporting woman."

"They call them that in the South, too," the police officer said.

"She's blonde, with blue eyes and about five-foot-four inches tall," Dix said.

"That's half the sporting women in town," the police officer said. "I can give you a hand looking."

"Wearing that uniform?" Dix said.

"My shift ends at midnight," the police officer said. "Give me a minute to change and I'll join you. Two looks less inconspicuous than one and I know the saloons better than you."

Dix rolled and smoked a cigarette while the police officer went inside the police station to change. He emerged a few minutes later wearing a suit and derby hat. His firearm was in a shoulder holster.

"Shall we go?" he said.

They visited seven more saloons and bars during the next two hours without success. Then, in the eighth saloon, a place on Chartres Street, as Dix and the police officer nursed shots of whiskey at the bar, Dix heard her voice coming from a room on the balcony.

"What's your name?" Dix said.

"Levine."

"Well, Mr. Levine, prepare to meet Miss Angela Wells," Dix said.

"Dix, followed by Levine, walked to the stairs that led to the balcony. A burly bouncer holding a club blocked the stairs.

"Federal officer," Dix said. "I have a warrant for the arrest of one of your girls. Kindly step aside."

A man appeared behind Dix. "Problem?' he said.

"Who are you?" Dix said.

"I own this establishment," the man said.

"I have a warrant for the arrest of one of your girls," Dix said.

"And you are?" the man said.

"Federal Warrant Officer," Dix said.

"May I see the warrant?" the man said.

Dix handed him the warrant. The man read it, returned it to Dix and nodded to the bouncer. The bouncer moved to allow Dix and Levine to pass.

Dix and Levine ascended the stairs. Angel's voice was coming from the second room. Dix opened the door and he and Levine entered the room. Angel was naked, talking to a man in bed.

Dix looked at the man. "Don't get up," he said.

Angel looked at Dix. "Aw, shit," she said.

"Get dressed," Dix said.

"Thanks for the use of your jail," Dix said.

"The captain will be in by eight," Levine said. "He'll want to talk to you. I should be there as well."

"Do you have a U.S. Marshal nearby?" Dix said.

"Right up the street," Levine said.

"Invite him as well," Dix said.

"See you in the morning," Levine said.

"Thanks for the help," Dix said.

Chapter Sixty-Nine

"It's beautiful," Trixie said as she and Pickford stood on the front porch.

"Mrs. Dix, how do you like the corral?" Mitchell said as he approached the porch.

"It's all so nice," Trixie said.

"The bunkhouse is finished," Mitchell said. "Come have a look."

Trixie and Pickford went with Mitchell to the bunkhouse. It was forty-feet-long, held twelve bunks, a large dining table, a woodstove for cooking, another for heat, a sink with a pump and an icebox for cold storage. The white trim gave it a homey look.

"Mr. Mitchell, you and your crew have done an exceptional job," Trixie said.

"Thank you, ma'am," Mitchel said. "We shall be done with the barn in two days."

"Mr. Mitchel, if I may, when you are done I would like to give you a five-hundred-dollar bonus to divide up with your men," Trixie said.

"You are most gracious, Mr. Dix," Mitchel said.

"Now, if you will excuse us, the Judge and I have to return to town and buy furniture," Trixie said.

Captain Parmetier, Levine, U.S. Marshal Gil Bellows and Dix met in Parmetier's office on the second floor of the police station.

"Marshal Bellows, I leave it to you to transport Miss Wells to Washington DC, where she will be held without bail until trial," Dix said.

"We can handle that," Bellows said.

"Let's go talk to Miss Wells," Dix said.

Angel was seated at a table in the interview room. She had a cup of coffee and was smoking a cigarette.

"The gang's all here," she said.

"Where is Marty?" Dix said.

"Why should I tell you a damn thing?" Angel said.

"Because if you do, you'll be charged with robbery and assault," Dix said. "And if you don't, you'll be charged with murder."

"Murder? Did the Judge die from a pinky wound?" Angel smirked.

"No, but Trixie's unborn baby did," Dix said.

Angel sat up straight. Her eyes closed for a moment. Then she opened her eyes and said, "That was all Marty. You can't pin that on me."

"What did he do, dump you here and take off with the Judge's money?" Dix said.

"I didn't know she was pregnant," Angel said. "You can't blame me for that."

"If I take my gun and fire a bullet through the wall and it kills somebody in the next room, I didn't mean to kill him, but he's just as dead," Dix said. "So what's it going to be, seven years out in five, or life?"

"That son of a bitch Marty," Angel said. "Yeah, he skipped out on me alright. Took the money and left me dry."

"Where did he go?" Dix said.

"Not so fast," Angel said. "I want some assurances I won't be slapped with a murder charge."

Dix removed an envelope from his pocket. "I had the police chief and marshal Bellows witness this statement from me," he said. "If you want my signature, tell me where he is."

"I can tell you where he went," Angel said.

"So, tell me," Dix said.

"Marty, that asshole. He fancies himself a New Orleans gentleman," Angel said. "He went off to gamble on a Mississippi Riverboat."

"Which one?" Dix said.

"I don't know and that's the truth," Angel said. "But I can tell you this, he'll gamble until he's rich or broke."

"Captain, have you a pen?" Dix said.

"Where can I get one of these floating gambling houses?" Dix said.

"Best bet is Saint Louis," Captain Parmetier said. "But there's a half dozen of such gambling ships sailing the Mississippi for pleasure. Each carrying hundreds of passengers."

"It's a long shot at best," Levine said.

"It's the best chance I have," Dix said. "Marshal Bellows, I leave Miss Wells in your capable hands. Officer Levine, thank you for your help."

"Good luck," Levine said. "We'll take care of your horse.

"About that," Dix said. "Just don't try to ride him."

Chapter Seventy

Using several catalogues at the general store, Trixie ordered bedroom furniture for the four bedrooms, Pickford picking out his own. Then they selected furniture for the kitchen, living room, study, parlor, pantry and bathing room. Last came furniture for the front and back porches.

The everyday dishes, pots and pans and cutlery, Trixie purchased at the general store. The dishes and cutlery for holidays and special occasions, she ordered from the catalogues.

"We spent three-thousand-dollars today," Trixie said.

"Every penny well spent," Pickford said. "Now, let's spend a little more on supper."

Dix caught the six PM train to Saint Louis that was scheduled to arrive at eight in the morning.

Before leaving New Orleans, he sent a

telegram to Trixie and Pickford in care of the Carson City hotel. He also purchased a book to read titled, The Adventures of Tom Sawyer by someone named Mark Twain.

Dix read while he ate dinner and then through most of the night and finished the book before the train arrived in Saint Louis.

From the train station, Dix took a taxi to the pier where the riverboats boarded. One was in port, the New Orleans, and was scheduled to leave at six PM. The ship was not designed to transport passengers from one place to another.

It was strictly pleasure cruising, with dining, gambling, entertainment and every kind of liquor imaginable.

Dix purchased a ticket for a stateroom. The first thing he did was sleep.

He woke up around four in the afternoon, shaved and washed up and changed into the suit he brought for traveling. Then he took a walk around the ship. It was designed for luxury and was at full capacity of two-hundred passengers.

Most were huddled in groups in various rooms and lounges. Dix looked at the faces of the male passengers. The casino and card room were closed until the ship left port.

The dining room was open, though not full and Dix, having missed breakfast and lunch, decided on an early dinner.

At six o'clock, he went on deck with all the other passengers as the ship set sail. He returned to his room to pocket the two-shot, .45 caliber Derringer he kept in his satchel, then went to the casino.

Every gaming table was occupied. Dix got a whiskey from a hostess and watched faces. He only met Marty a handful of times at the saloon, but Dix would never forget his face and voice.

Dix checked the rooms reserved for cards. Every tabled was occupied, but Marty was present.

At nine o'clock, there was live entertainment in the main hall. There was a banjo and guitar player, a piano and horn and a female singer. Dix watched for a few minutes, lost interest and returned to the main casino.

If Marty was on board, he was in his stateroom.

Dix went topside and found a chair near the bow, rolled a smoked a cigarette. With full capacity, the New Orleans wouldn't stop until it reached Springfield and after that, Saint Paul, where it would turn around and head back to New Orleans.

Dix waited until midnight and then returned to the casino and card game rooms.

There was no sign of Marty. He wasn't on board ship.

Levine's words came to mind. 'It's a long shot at best.'

But the only hand Dix had.

CHAPTER SEVENTY-ONE

Trixie and Pickford were having breakfast at the Carson City Hotel when a desk clerk brought them a telegram.

"It's from Dix," Pickford said. "He's arrested Angel and she's being transported to Washington to stand trial."

"What about Marty?" Trixie said.

"Dix is on his way to Saint Louis," Pickford said.

"Why?"

"He doesn't say," Pickford said. "But I wouldn't bet against your husband for any money."

In Springfield, fifty passengers exited the New Orleans and were replaced by another fifty. Half of the fifty were men. None of the men were Marty.

Days later, in Saint Paul, all two-hundred passengers got off the ship and were replaced by another group of two-hundred.

Dix spent the better part of the morning on the pier, watching every male passenger enter the New Orleans.

There was another luxury steamboat headed south, the Enterprise. Dix booked a stateroom and spent the afternoon sleeping.

The Enterprise left port at six PM. After two days on the Mississippi River, Dix knew that Marty wasn't on board.

The freight company needed four large wagons to deliver the furniture to the house. Trixie knew exactly where everything went and by the end of the day, the house was fully furnished.

"Judge, after all that hotel food, how about a homecooked meal for a change?" Trixie said.

"I thought you would never ask," Pickford said.

In Springfield, half the passengers got off the Enterprise and were replaced by a like amount. None of them were Marty.

The rest of the trip to Saint Louis was uneventful.

In port was the steamship the Washington, another pleasure cruise paddleboat. Dix booked a stateroom and boarded in the early afternoon.

He didn't bother checking the ship and took a long nap in his room. When he awoke, she shaved, washed up and dressed carefully, tucking the Derringer into a pocket before he left the room.

The Enterprise had left port and the passengers were in full activity, gambling, eating and drinking.

Dix grabbed a bite to eat and then went to the casino. Half the passengers were at gaming tables, of which half were men.

By midnight, Dix knew Marty wasn't on board.

Dix left the Enterprise in Saint Paul. He stood on the pier with luggage in hand and looked at the paddle boat called the Mississippi Queen. A large banner was stretched across the bow.

Poker Championship 25,000 First Prize.

Chapter Seventy-Two

"Judge, are you going to try the case against Angel and Marty when Dix finds him?" Trixie said.

"I can't," Pickford said. "I'm the victim, along with you. However, our testimony is sure to get him hung."

Trixie nodded. "I need to go to town today," she said. "We need to stock up the pantry."

"I'll hitch up the buggy," Pickford said.

The Mississippi Queen was the largest and most luxurious steam-powered, paddleboat on the river. Capacity was three hundred guests. The casino was huge, the private card game rooms were also larger, there were two dining halls and a theater for live entertainment.

The tournament was limited to one-hundred players, man or woman, with an entry fee of one-thousand-dollars. The tournament would start when the Queen left Saint Paul and end in Saint Louis.

First prize was twenty-five-thousand dollars. There was no second prize. Security on board was tight, with armed guards in every room. A disclaimer stated that any man or woman caught cheating would be put overboard or arrested. The choice was theirs.

A ticket for a room on this special voyage was one-hundred-dollars. Dix purchased a ticket at which time he was asked if he was a player or a spectator. He told them he was a spectator.

The first thing Dix did was go to his stateroom and take a much needed nap. Then he shaved, washed and dressed in his suit, pocketed the Derringer and warrant and then went to one of the dining halls for dinner.

They were six hours outside of Saint Paul. After dinner, Dix went to the main casino, which was almost empty.

Most of the passengers were in the card rooms, watching the tournament. Marty wasn't in the first card room.

He was, however, in the second.

There were ten tables with five players, plus a dealer at each table. Marty was at table three. He was dressed as a southern gentlemen and smoked a cigar as he sipped whiskey.

Dix stood back with the crowd and watched the game progress. Marty was a decent enough player, but had little chance of winning the tournament. One, because he wasn't good enough and two, because he was about to be arrested.

The player opposite Marty stood up to take a break.

Dix removed his badge and held it in his left hand. Then he walked forward, stepped up onto the chair vacated by the player, then stepped onto the table and looked at Marty.

Shock silenced the room.

Dix held up his badge for all to see. "United States Federal Warrant Officer, "he said. "And this is official business."

"How the fu . . . ?" Marty said.

Dix kicked Marty in the face, knocking him and the chair over.

"I have a federal warrant," Dix said and jumped down from the table. Marty, face bloody, was about to sit up when Dix kicked him again. "For the arrest of Martin Kovac for . . ."

Marty rolled onto his belly and started to crawl away. Dix stuck his right foot on Marty's back. "For robbery, assault, battery, rape and murder," Dix said.

The ship's captain and three armed officers surrounded Dix. “May I see the warrant?” the captain said.

Dix removed the warrant from his pocket and handed it to the captain. He read the warrant and returned it to Dix.

“Captain, do you have a jail on board?” Dix said.

The captain turned to his three officers. “Take him to the brig,” he said. “Mr. Dix, would you come with me please?”

The captain handed Dix a glass of whiskey and then poured one for himself. “Why didn’t you alert me first before you disrupted the game?” he said.

“This one was personal for me, captain,” Dix said. “He robbed a federal judge and cut a finger off his left hand and he is a close friend of mine. The woman he raped is my wife and the murder was of our unborn child.”

“I see,” the captain said. “I can certainly understand you wanting to make the arrest yourself.”

“We’ll be getting off in Springfield,” Dix said.

“I’ll arrange it so you and the prisoner are escorted off first,” the captain. “In the meantime, I hope you enjoy the ship.”

“I will now,” Dix said.

Chapter Seventy-Three

"It's been ten days since the last telegram," Trixie said as she and Pickford walked the streets of Carson City.

"I've often said this, but it's worth repeating," Pickford said. "What Dix does is the toughest job in law enforcement. Unlike any other law enforcement branch, Dix works alone and that in itself makes his job more difficult. And dangerous. The point is that he doesn't always have the time to send telegrams."

"Are you trying to tell me to be patient?" Trixie said.

"Remember what I taught you about chess?" Pickford said.

They reached the general store. "I won't be long," Trixie said.

"I'm going to the post office," Pickford said. "I'll meet you back here shortly."

Trixie entered the general store, Pickford continued on to the post office. His mail from Washington was forwarded and included in the stack was a telegram from Dix.

"I'm afraid the money recovered that belongs to Judge Pickford won't be returned until after the trial," the Attorney General said. "Unfortunately, Kovac spent six-thousand."

"That won't be a problem," Dix said.

"We'll notify you in plenty of time before the trial starts," the Attorney General said.

"Thanks," Dix said.

"Tell the Judge, we all miss him," the Attorney General said.

"I will," Dix said.

Levine accompanied Dix to the livery where Dix's horse was stabled. The horse was very excited to see Dix and showed it by whinnying and stomping his front hooves. Dix calmed the horse down by gently rubbing his neck.

"You got your man, now what?" Levine said.

"I'm talking my horse and going home," Dix said. "And starting a ranch."

Chapter Seventy-Four

Trixie and Pickford were planting rose bushes along the front of the house under the porch. After several hours of digging and planting, they took a break with some cool lemonade and sat in chairs on the porch.

"Dix is coming," Pickford said.

"When?" Trixie said.

"Right now. See?" Pickford said and pointed to a tiny dot on the horizon.

"That could be anybody," Trixie said.

"He sent a telegram from Saint Louis that he would be home today," Pickford said.

"And you didn't tell me this?" Trixie said.

"If I had, it wouldn't be much of a surprise, now would it," Pickford said.

Trixie's hair was a mess. Her face and hands were covered with dirt. So were her riding pants and blouse. And she didn't care. She stepped down off the porch and walked towards the dot on the horizon that was Dix.

She walked about a hundred yards and then could clearly see Dix on his massive horse. Her heart was pounding as she broke into a run. Dix raced his horse toward her.

They met somewhere in the middle.

"You look homeless," Dix said from the saddle.

"That's the sweetest thing anybody ever said to me," Trixie said.

"Want a ride?" Dix said.

"I don't accept rides from strangers," Trixie said.

"In that case, I'll walk along with you," Dix said and slid down from the saddle.

"People call me Dix," Dix said.

"Trixie."

"There, we're not strangers anymore," Dix said.

"I don't kiss on the first date," Trixie said.

"Consider this our second date," Dix said and took hold of Trixie.

While Trixie took a bath, Dix and Pickford drank coffee on the porch. Dix rolled and lit a cigarette.

"The place looks beautiful," Dix said. "I like the roses."

"Trixie's idea," Pickford said. "She wants some in front of the bunkhouse, too."

"You've both done a hell of a job, Judge," Dix said.

"Mostly her," Pickford said.

"I met some cattle buyers in Dallas a while back," Dix said. "As soon as the trial is over, let's head down and buy some."

"We'll be close enough," Pickford said.

"Judge, Washington is twelve-hundred miles from Dallas," Dix said.

"Remember my old friend Judge Parker?" Pickford said.

"The Hanging Judge, sure," Dix said.

"While you were off prancing around, I . . ." Pickford said.

"Prancing?" Dix said.

"I made arrangements for their trial to be held in Fort Smith, with Parker presiding," Pickford said.

"Can Parker do that?" Dix said.

"He's a Federal Judge, same as me," Pickford said.

"Well, isn't that just too bad for them," Dix said.

ABOUT THE AUTHOR

Al Lamanda was born in The Bronx, New York, and lived most of his life in Manhattan. His debut novel *Dunston Falls* received high praise from *Kirkus* and *Publishers Weekly* and from there he was hooked, writing more than twenty novels and several screenplays.

The employees of Thorndike Press hope you have enjoyed this Large Print book. All our Thorndike Large Print titles are designed for easy reading, and all our books are made to last. Other Thorndike Press Large Print books are available at your library, through selected bookstores, or directly from us.

For information about titles, please call:
(800) 223-1244

or visit our website at:
gale.com/thorndike

www.ingramcontent.com/pod-product-compliance
Lightning Source LLC
Jackson TN
JSHW082336140826
106627JS00006B/9